80 Stories High

Uplifting tales of humble heroes

By Dr John Irvine Paediatric Psychologist
Editorial Comments by Richard Lornie OAM

A catalogue record for this
work is available from the
National Library of Australia

Disclaimer

Many of the ideas in this book are reflections on cases in the author's Clinic going back many years. As such, they may depict cultural biases, genders, roles, situations and stereotypes which are unacceptable today. Our culture is evolving and we can learn and grow from past perceptions and mistakes. The stories are not intended as medical advice nor prescribe the use of any techniques as a form of treatment for any problems physical, psychological or other. The author apologises if any of the suggestions or quotes, in becoming part of the tribal wisdom, directly replicate unacknowledged sources. Although the 80 stories are based on fact and pay homage to the author's heroes, in many cases the author has had to de-identify names, location and other details to protect the privacy of the individual and/or where circumstance precluded obtaining publishing permission. If any offence is caused, please accept the author's humble apology. The celebrity stories are inspirational and insightful about personalities probably known best for their professional contribution. Permission was sought and granted for their inclusion in a previous publication, "Who'd Be A Parent: The Manual That Should Have Come With The Kids". These extracts are respectfully reproduced here verbatim. The author also wishes to dissociate the READ clinic, Wonderful Me or the WorryWoos from any of the material contained in the book.

To My Humble Hero

_____

Dedication

Written in my 80th year, "80 Stories High" is deliberately intended to convey the breath-taking heights of my gratitude for a fortunate life and to reflect on 80 of the humble heroes who have enriched it. Originally inspired by my friend Angela Barrett who wanted to write my biography, I felt it was time to change the focus and salute some of the amazing people I've met on my journey before the memories fade. The added impetus is that our family, like so many other families, has been affected by Dementia but one thing I can do is dedicate proceeds from the book to Dementia research.

At the outset, let me say that this book would never have seen daylight without a very talented team's incredible and voluntary support. I thank Richard, the overseeing Editor; Judy, the wonderful nit-picker and quality controller; Stan, my old wise mate and book draft reader; and Andi Green, the creator, illustrator and owner of the WorryWoos.

And now, at long last, I get to dedicate this book of love-based stories to the wonderful women in my life – many I've worked alongside and others who have so humbly and efficiently glued us all together with love. I especially want to acknowledge my mum, Helen; my wife, Jean; and my three beautiful daughters, Jenny, Heather and Rosie. I also want to recognise our amazing grandchildren – Brodie, Barney, Jensen, Manon, Luca and Madeleine. Thank you so much. This book is my legacy to you all.

Foreword

Life is a miraculous accident over which we have limited control. We're born, we breathe, we're buffeted, and as we get off the hurdy-gurdy we take a breather. That's where I am and why this book had to happen. In a way, it's like spinning my professional cocoon as I adjust to life post-retirement. My hearing difficulties may render me past my clinic and media prime but the good news is that my memories are so rich, my gratitude so overwhelming and my need to continue to give back so strong that it's just a lateral move rather than a slippery downward slide.

The other trigger for this book has been the overwhelming need for good news stories. We're inundated and overloaded with bad news stories every day and in every marketable way. Humanity survives not on this constant arousal of The Sympathetic Nervous System but on good news, faith, love, courage, resilience and belief in each other's potential for good. Only then can we breathe easier and engage our Parasympathetic Nervous System, allowing us to calm down and relax.

These are stories of ordinary humble people restoring our faith, hope and love for each other. Just a bit about the stories:

- They're all true stories, but I've had to change names and details to protect the innocent and de-identify individuals where needed (unless they're famous).

- I've tried to use the contributions of famous people interspersed among my own stories in every series.

- Although I haven't advertised my stories or the Humble Hero podcasts, I've been getting some feedback from listeners/readers acknowledging their unsung heroes. I value these stories so much, and I have interspersed these, too, among my own stories. My not-so-secret hope is that someone will promote these contributions publicly so that other editions can emerge long after the fickle finger of fate has crooked its digit my way.

- In my mind, the stories are meant to be read at the end of the day after the daily battles for bread have been fought and, win or lose, we dedicate time to put those battles behind us and snuggle into some good news.

Series 1

1. Nada – an incredible story about Grandma Nada becoming the surrogate for her daughter who couldn't have children

2. Andrew – exchange student Andy faces his demons in another country

3. Barbara – Grandma Barbara shows her ingenuity in beating a problem with trichotillomania

4. Brodie – my shameful and rather unorthodox clinical methods get results

5. Charlotte – young Charlotte shows what resilience and courage are all about

6. Elena – WorryWoo Rue comes to Elena's rescue and salvages her self-image

7. Podcast listener's humble hero: Bill – Richard shares his story on his ex-father-in-law Bill and his lesson in forgiveness

8. Sidney – late bloomers can sometimes show us that when life blocks our first choices, the side or back door can produce even better results

9. Julie – Julie was worried about her body shape but decided that she would like herself anyway

10. Celebrity contribution: Jeannie Little – often the most successful adults have had to rise above childhood setbacks. This famous lady gives us a lesson in doing it tough

Story 1

Nada

An incredible story about Grandma Nada
becoming the surrogate for her daughter who
couldn't have children

*N*ada works as a fitness instructor at our local gym. She was in her fifties, so you can imagine my surprise when I noticed the unmistakable pregnancy bump, but it was none of my business, so I left it at that. Then Nada took pregnancy leave, and I didn't see her for many months. This is her story as she conveyed it to me on her return to the gym.

Two years earlier, Nada learned that her daughter couldn't have children as her uterus was not fully formed. However, as Nada's daughter had viable eggs, an option was surrogacy.

The family didn't dare trust an overseas surrogate, so they thought they were stumped. However, Nada's research indicated that post-menopausal women could become surrogates. She contacted the IVF clinic, and they agreed to take her on.

Then began the two long, arduous years of preparing Nada's uterus with oestrogen and progesterone so that it could carry the embryo. Of course, they also had to go through the legal and psychological hoops before the authorities finalised a contract.

With that behind them and the legal green light, now began the long process of extracting seven eggs, five of which were successfully created into embryos using her son-in-law's semen. Due to the external semen use, these embryos needed to be quarantined for four months in case of any infectious diseases.

The medical team then selected the most viable embryo, after which they had to wait ten days to see whether the transfer had succeeded. Success! Can you imagine Nada's feelings? Not only was she carrying her own grandchild, but she also experienced the overwhelming realisation that she was helping to create a family that would not have been possible if it wasn't for her!

The night before the due date, Nada and daughter bunkered down in the hospital, ready for induction. To their relief and delight, the baby was born hale and hearty, and the daughter and husband now had a family.

But not content with that, ten months later, the family repeated the exercise and another healthy little sister was born.

I'm sure Nada could have publicised this incredible story in magazines and top-rating TV shows, but Nada is a true humble hero. She just says it was literally a labour of love! It's not quite a fairy tale ending because her daughter and family live far away in a large country town. But she does see them, and they are still gob-smacked at the whole exercise and its life-giving outcome.

As a male, I find it hard to fathom the depths of such love, to not only go through so much to bring another human to life, let alone repeat the process another generation later, but then nurture the offspring for the rest of your life. And to every mum, no matter what mistakes you may have made in the process, you offer a glimpse at the ageless edge of eternity.

Editorial comment:
I share Dr John's awe at the power of a mother's love and what it can accomplish.
"I am sure that if the mothers of various nations could meet, there would be no more wars."
– E. M. Forster

Story 2

Andrew

Exchange student Andy faces his demons in
another country

Of all the young adults I have ever met, this Japanese boy, Asami (but he calls himself Andrew), left his mark big-time. Andrew was a Japanese student who left home at sixteen after suffering severe depression and a nervous breakdown.

Andrew wanted to get as far away from his past as possible and make a new start, so he came to Australia, determined to be a different person and not let the black dog of depression bite again. He worked hard, walked, exercised, learned to play golf, bought a motorbike and was one of the most popular Japanese students the school had ever had.

Although the black dog disappeared, Andrew lived with this enormous fear that the black dog would bite again when he returned to Japan after completing the HSC.

Fortunately, Andrew was billeted out with the best host family anyone would ever want. They loved Andrew like a son, and their 13-year-old son, Luke, absolutely adored him. Then fate played its hand. Just a couple of months later into his stay, young Luke was shot in the stomach by feral teenagers out for a bit of shooting practice in the local park where Luke was playing with Andrew and another mate. It was only an air gun pellet, but it was delicately wedged in his stomach, and his condition was serious.

The family were naturally angry and distressed, which was the trigger to bring Andrew undone again. Back came the tight tummies and depression.

The day Luke came out of the hospital, Andrew's pain lifted overnight and has not returned. Andrew stayed to complete his exams, then returned to Japan with a very proud dad who flew out from Japan to thank us all and take Andrew home. Andrew brought his dad in to meet me before he left, and I must admit to being very choked up as I said my goodbyes and warned him that he must look deep inside himself to prevent such a catastrophic recurrence.

He grinned broadly, "Ah, but Dr John, I finally have. You see," he said, "it took Luke's injury to show me what I was doing wrong. I was wearing other people's pain. I was climbing their mountains for them. Back in Japan, when my mother or father was stressed, I would wear it, and that was not good because I could not solve their problems for them. If I just climb my mountain, I know in my heart that I can be strong when people need me. I am ready to go back home now. I have finally found my answer."

Then on his way out of my office, he called back with a cheeky grin on his face, "I will call you if I am in trouble. When we're down, we all need someone who believes in us. Dr John, why don't you start a "dial-a-grandparent service?"

So, home the proud pair were headed back to a new life, but not empty-headed or empty-handed. Not only did Andy learn a good lesson, but he also taught us all a few on the way. Sayonara, Asami.

Editorial comment:
It must be difficult for exchange students like Asami to first adjust to life in a foreign country and then have to adjust all over again when they go home. I am full of admiration for their resilience and strength of character. Shawn Achor's advice applies not only to exchange students but to us as well.

"Take impeccable care of your health. Eating well and getting plenty of exercise and sleep are critical to keeping stress at bay. So too is practising gratitude…it gives you a storehouse of positives to help neutralise and counterbalance any negatives."
– Shawn Achor

Story 3

Barbara

Grandma Barbara shows her ingenuity in
beating a problem with trichotillomania

Barbara was a very spritely grandparent who filled her grandchildren's lives with joy. Her house was always busy and smelt good and appetising. Whenever the grandkids were over, they'd make cakes or brownies – and when her vegan daughter was visiting, Barbara would make a chicken veggie pie for those meat-deprived grandkids! Every reader would have had, or wish they'd had, someone like Barbara in their childhood.

But one particular grandchild had her worried. Young Olivia was a gorgeous four-year-old, very bright and well-adjusted, but she suffered from trichotillomania! Olivia had become an involuntary hair-puller! She would put her left hand over her head to twirl her hair into a single strand and then pull it out. Olivia only did it when she was tired or in bed while she sucked her thumb. As her hairline started receding from over her right ear, Olivia kept following it, and the bald strip above the right ear became more obvious.

Her parents had talked to her about it and had tried Rescue Remedy, thinking it was a stress thing. They had reminded her, cajoled her, and even tried a sharp "Ah, ah" when they caught Olivia doing it in front of the TV. They had even changed her hairstyle to try and hide the erosion, all to no avail.

But they hadn't tried Grandma's ingenuity! Among her many talents, Barbara was also a great knitter, so she and I got our heads together to solve this family crisis! We knew that Olivia loved Santa, and Barbara decided to exploit that opportunity as we headed towards Christmas. She made a special bonnet for Olivia to wear to bed. This bonnet, which was held in place with bobby pins, not only had Christmas colours but also had Rudolph's red nose sewn onto the top of the bonnet as a pom-pom.

Grandma had convinced Olivia that the other reindeer were looking where to deliver presents and were attracted to Rudolph's red nose, so if Olivia wore the bonnet every night, the reindeer would know where to call. Olivia's parents also put the yukky nail-bite deterrent on Olivia's thumb to try and get a disconnect between the automatic thumb sucking when tired and the hair pulling. The combination worked wonders, and Olivia followed Grandma's brilliant scheme.

And Barbara enjoyed the exercise too. Barbara's motto was, "We're never too old to enjoy our childhood!" Grandparent she may have been biologically, but in her heart, she was still the wondering child, loving the joy of Christmas.

By the way, Barbara said the trickiest part of the operation was answering Olivia's question, "But Grandma, wouldn't the reindeer know to come to our house when they saw our Christmas tree?"

"Oh no," she retorted, "It's Rudolph's red nose that attracts them." And Olivia, aged four, let Barbara get away with that reply because Nana was perfect!

So, what's the message? If you want to get on well with kids, think like a kid.

Robert Brault is reputed to have written these words, "Today, I bent the truth to be kind, and I have no regret, for I am far surer of what is kind than I am of what is true."

Editorial comment:
I like this story and I like the message, but most of all I like Barbara. She's the sort of spritely Grandma every child deserves to have in their life.

"We don't stop playing because we grow old. We grow old because we stop playing."
– George Bernard Shaw

Story 4

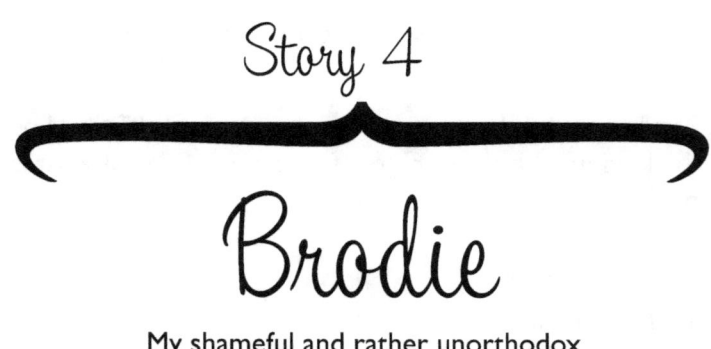

Brodie

My shameful and rather unorthodox
clinical methods get results

They say that "experience" is an acceptable noun we give to our mistakes. Maybe this story falls into that category.

Brodie was a 14-year-old problem. He had been sent into the Clinic by a children's services agency for stealing and not just once. Brodie was an inveterate kleptomaniac. His dad had died tragically and his poor mum had four kids to rear, with Brodie being the eldest. Brodie was lonely and role-model rudderless. I often find compulsive stealing is taking with the hand what is missing from the heart.

Anyhow, Brodie and his mum came into my consulting room, and after the three of us chatted, mum went out to the waiting room and Brodie and I got to know each other. We got on well, and we talked about his dad and the ache in Brodie's heart. I thought we made good progress so I set up an action plan for mum and Brodie. That plan included the idea that mum would leave money lying around somewhere every day, and it was Brodie's job to walk past it repeatedly and not touch it. We also set up some trust goals at school with the Year Coordinator.

Brodie returned a few weeks later, and mum was grinning from ear to ear. The school had reported significant progress and nothing was missing from home or her bag. I was surprised as we had only met once and the problem was chronically compulsive. However, I accepted mum's thanks. I called Brodie in and we discussed progress and our plan. Brodie went out into the waiting room, and I asked mum back in to keep her in the treatment loop.

As I was ushering mum out, my secretary, Lynne, whispered to me between gritted teeth, "The money is missing from the till!" Smiling at Lynne, as one should when in the public eye, I gritted back, "How can the money be missing from the till?" To which she gritted back, "I had to go to the toilet, didn't I? When I came back, it was gone".

By this stage, mum and Brodie were heading happily for the door. With only metres to spare till they hit the exit, I called out to mum and asked if I could see Brodie for a minute as there was something else I needed to check on.

With that, a reluctant Brodie shuffled into my room. I closed the door, stood (or to be honest, shoved) him against the wall and put it to Brodie that I knew he had our money in his pockets, so here was the deal. If he were to confess and "cough up", I wouldn't tell his mum or the school (as the school had taken him off the daily behaviour report because he had "improved" so much). Brodie agreed, handed back the till money, and we parted company.

I never saw Brodie or his mum again. Well, that's not quite true. Years later, as I was getting a police kerb-side breath test, this young officer looked at my licence and asked me whether I was the Dr John, who was a "kids' Psych". I owned up to that fact, and he said, "Doc, you won't remember me, but my name is Brodie, and you saw me when I was a kid when I was in a bit of trouble at school for stealing".

How could I ever forget!! "Yes," he said, "You taught me a big lesson then. I was starting to enjoy having playground time again, and poor old mum was so proud of me. I didn't want to let her down, so here I am!" My mouth just gaped. If ever I was sure my therapeutic strategies had been found wanting then this case was it!

In fact my therapy techniques were so unprofessional that I probably could have faced disciplinary action if the truth be known. My point is that sometimes we make mistakes, sometimes big ones, but just being genuine may prove to be the best teacher. I learnt a big lesson that day, not only to never leave the till unattended, but about the incredible power of a mother's love. The trust of a mum is probably the best curfew and behaviour manager any teenage boy can have. To Brodie's mum, Mrs Mac, welcome to the Humble Heroes' Hall of Fame.

Editorial comment:
We all make mistakes. Bill Gates once said, "It's fine to celebrate success but it is more important to heed the lessons of failure". Dr John worried about his unorthodox technique in dealing with Brodie but the lesson was a very positive one, worthy of celebrating.

"The real religion of the world comes from women much more than from men – from mothers most of all, who carry the key to our souls in their bosoms."
– Oliver Wendell Holmes Sr

Story 5

Charlotte

Young Charlotte shows what resilience
and courage are all about

$\mathcal{I}$'ve known Charlotte for most of her 13 years on this earth – a chatty, lively girl who lived locally.

Charlotte was such a chatterbox, usually about some make-believe topic, that the other girls just smirked at each other and moved away. Her parents were very loving, but it was obvious to everyone, except the school, that she was struggling academically – way behind in basic skills and left behind socially by her more mature friends. So it was understandable that Charlotte was trying to avoid school – she felt she was a failure in the classroom and a failure in the playground.

Her Grandma was a music teacher, and when the school formed a band Gran leased out one of the clarinets – and every day she would listen to Charlotte play in her room or over the phone. Charlotte showed some promise, so Gran paid for private lessons and this year managed to get her included in the local woodwind group.

But Charlotte's most significant asset was her acrobatic ability. Her mum had noticed that she was constantly bouncing and jumping, so they got her into a cheerleading group. Charlotte was so slight and lithe that she soon became one of the group's high performers. She was the kid lifted to the apex of the formation. Last year they won 1st at Nationals and in the State.

This term, the teacher asked every student in her class to prepare a three minute speech about a topic of their choice. Charlotte was keen to talk about her cheerleading, so with her Grandad's help wrote a story called, "A Loser No More". She practised and practised until she could read it fluently. It started by saying, "Most of you know that I'm not very good at spelling or reading or maths or writing. I suppose you could call me a big-time loser." Then she went on to say how she found cheerleading and how well her team had done and then finished up along the lines, "Although I wish I were better at schoolwork, at least I'm good at something. Everyone can be a winner if you find what you're good at, just keep trying and never give up."

Just recently, Charlotte had a thorough intellectual and educational assessment – the results were not comforting, down in the bottom one percent intellectually and over three years behind in basic skills – her parents and family were devastated. Still, I have been at pains to reassure them that Charlotte will always find a job and succeed because although her IQ may be low, her EQ (Emotional Intelligence) is way up there. Charlotte truly is a champion – she has the resilience, courage and self-belief that will make her a winner in life no matter the setbacks. Well done, Charlotte!

And Gran, if you're reading this, welcome to the Humble Heroes' Hall of Fame – you may feel at times that your spirits are sagging, but you've unleashed an energy in Charlotte that will be ongoing.

Editorial comment:
In our dealings with others, IQ isn't worth much without the influence of EQ. We aren't as smart as we think we are if we can't be kind to others.

"Too often we underestimate the power of a touch, a smile, a kind word, a listening ear, or the smallest act of caring, all of which have the potential to turn a life around."
– Leo Buscaglia

Story 6

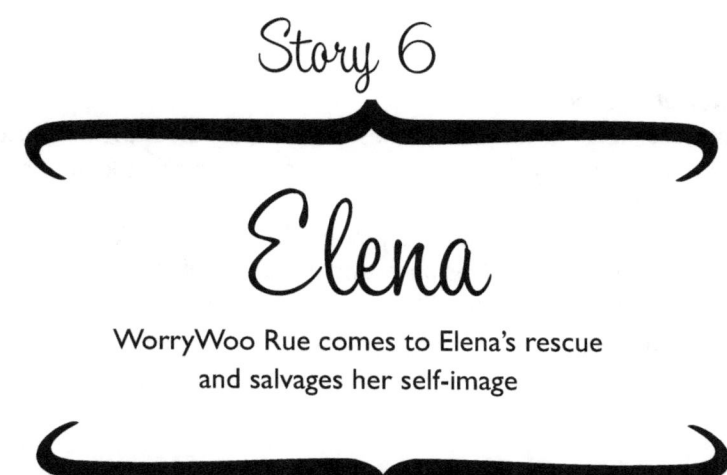

Elena

WorryWoo Rue comes to Elena's rescue
and salvages her self-image

Do you have favourite memories of toys from your childhood? I'm wondering whether Rue will always occupy that special place for Elena.

Young Elena was just six when her parents brought her in to see me – a bouncy, pixie sort of kid with big wide blue eyes, very fair skin, her hair tied back and with a fringe at the front. Her parents knew she was bright and was already reading "chapter" books and drawing whenever she got the chance, but this year at school, her grades, attitude and attendance had all gone downhill in a hurry. Bullying was the school's best bet, so they shifted her to another table with lovely kids, but nothing changed. Elena just said she hated school.

From countless years working with kids, I've found that if you want them to open up, take the spotlight off them, or they get too emotionally overheated – just engage their imagination, preferably using a third party that's not threatening. Sometimes I might use my magic gemstone rocks or some other little squeezable symbol to engage their imagination.

Elena was attracted to my WorryWoos characters sitting on the shelf behind me. These are very cuddly attractive dolls used a lot in schools as part of the SEL (Social and Emotional Literacy) program – and each character carries some emotional challenge – like worry or anger, jealousy, loneliness, insecurity, low self-esteem or confusion. To my surprise, Elena chose Rue, the one with self-image problems. Rue hated her big nose! So I let Elena take Rue home along with the storybook, "The Nose That Didn't Fit".

The following week, when Elena came back in, we talked about Rue and the fact that Rue didn't like herself because she had a big nose. I asked Elena if there was something about herself that she didn't like. Quick as a flash, Elena swept her fringe off her forehead, exposing an eczema rash on her hairline. To me it was the slightest blemish, but not to Elena. Her little eyes were glistening with grief so, to take the focus off her, I shared a few things I didn't like about my looks and then Elena's mum joined in with a few she didn't like about herself, and we all started laughing as we off-loaded our body image issues. It was great fun. Elena had no idea that mum hated her pale skin too! So, with the teacher's support, I let Elena take Rue and the book to school. The teacher and Elena were both surprised at how many kids didn't like something about their body – height, hair, skin, ears, teeth, nose – everything got a mention. When the teacher asked Elena, she quickly and confidently swept her hair back and named her eczema. No one in the class was all that interested as they each had their defect to mention, but it made Elena realise that we're all different, and that's what makes us realise who we are.

Elena's fine now. And she reinforced two fundamentals about human frailties — how oversensitive we are about anything that makes us feel different and how powerful play, especially with the inclusion of a third-party play object, is in unearthing and unwinding kids' problems.

Well done, Elena! I'm reminded of just how important toys are to kids. And I'm reminded of those words attributed to Desmond Morris, "Life is like a very short visit to a toy shop between birth and death. "

Editorial comment:
I love that quote from Desmond Morris. For a small child there is no division between playing and learning.

"It is in playing, and only in playing, that the individual child or adult is able to be creative and to use the whole personality, and it is only in being creative that the individual discovers the self. "
— D. W. Winnicott, Paediatrician

Story 7

Bill

Richard shares his story on his ex-father-in-law
Bill and his lesson in forgiveness

Podcast Listener's Humble Hero

$\mathcal{I}$'ve mentioned that in my "Humble Heroes" podcasts my grandson, Jensen, the editor, would throw open the option of people writing in with their Humble Hero. When I decided to print the stories, I asked Richard Lornie to do the editing and asked him to nominate someone who had greatly influenced him. This is his submission:

Dr John, you've asked for my contribution, and I need to tell you about my Humble Hero, Bill. I'm 76 years old now, but whenever I think of special people in my life, I just keep returning to Bill. He's no longer with us, but he profoundly influenced my life and those who met him.

Bill was a great entertainer. He loved hosting parties, and although, for the most part, he lived a solitary existence in his later years, he still was happy to have a barbecue or a dinner party to celebrate a special event.

If ever I had family visiting from overseas or an important visitor at the school, I would invite them to one of Bill's famous barbecues — after first checking with him that he was happy to be the host. There usually wasn't a problem, but when I suggested he host a barbecue for the Board Chairman and Headmaster of our sister school in Tokyo, he seemed disturbed at the prospect and barked, "Come with me". I followed him to his airy studio, where he kept all manner of particular objects, books, and paints. "See this?" He took a crudely made mess tin from a shelf. "I made this myself in Borneo. I used it for every meal in Sandakan and then Kuching."

Bill had fought in the infantry in Malaya in 1941/42 — the 2/30th. He was injured and, along with countless others involved in defence of Singapore, he ended up a prisoner of war in Changi. He was transferred to Sandakan and later moved to Kuching — a move that saved his life. Of 2,434 British and Australian troops held in Sandakan, only six were to survive, other than a group of officers who the Japanese moved to Kuching in October 1943. The remainder died on the infamous death marches to Ranau.

Unsurprisingly food was a constant preoccupation, and despite being severely malnourished, Bill and his mates often talked about food. Bill's homemade mess tin never saw a decent meal when he was a prisoner. The main ingredient in all the meals was the rice their captors issued to the men, and they managed to supplement this with greens smuggled into the camp.

Dressed only in makeshift jockstraps or loincloths, starving and ill, they sat and talked about restaurants they had visited. They spoke about meals they had eaten. They even played a game where one of the group would entertain the others with an account of a meal he would have when they eventually got back home to Australia. They spared no detail. The smells. The tastes. It was exquisite torture.

"So you want me to entertain your Japanese friends? Feed them? Be a generous host? I don't think I can do it, but leave it with me."

Bill did host the barbecue. It was a splendid affair with fillet steak, lamb chops and sausages. Bill served wine and beer. He regaled the guests with tales of his life and quizzed them about their knowledge of Australian wine, Australian artists and the Jazz scene of the Pre-War era.

The war was not mentioned until the very end. Bill didn't say much, only that he had been a prisoner of war. The guests looked dismayed, and I was worried that Bill would be upset, but he simply raised his glass, smiled, and proposed a simple toast. "Forgiveness – and love all round."

Dr John's comment:

I was fortunate enough to know Bill; he was everything Richard implied or mentioned – an amusing man, a scoundrel, a wonderful host and obviously a very resourceful man. And the thought of Bill and his mates sitting around soaking up memories of their favourite food at their favourite restaurants, while in reality, they soaked up soggy rice, is mind-blowing.

In other stories, we've mentioned the virtues of faith, hope and love. After all he went through in the Japanese prison camp, the forgiveness Bill showed certainly puts him right up there as a very worthy Humble Hero.

Story 8

Sidney

Late bloomers can sometimes show us that when life blocks our first choices, the side or back door can produce even better results

*A*re you what they call "a late bloomer"? According to Wikipedia, late bloomers do well because they have passion, resilience and persistence. They have had to rise above early setbacks (undetected sensory deficits, learning difficulties, ADHD, environmental limitations, family dysfunction, mindset, and social challenges, to name a few). Whatever the reason, many have not gone through the "front door" to success. They have had to go through a side door or even a back door to achieve their dreams. And how much sweeter it is when the battle has been so hard won? Setbacks are essential stepping stones to building resilience.

Sidney was one of my pin-up late bloomers. Sidney had learning difficulties. When I assessed him as an eight-year-old in the clinic, Sidney was already more than two years behind in reading, writing and spelling. He was already feeling the pain of classmates' putdowns for being dumb! To make matters worse, Sidney's sisters were all high achievers.

It was quite a sad meeting with Sidney's parents, both of whom were school teachers, and I recall their eyes glistening as they thought of the battles ahead for their youngest.

But like many other late bloomers, classroom measures of educational potential don't measure passion and determination, do they? Just as they poorly predicted other famous late bloomers such as Richard Branson, Lady Gaga, Winston Churchill, Bill Gates, Aretha Franklin, Stephen Spielberg, Ellen de Generes, and Oprah, to name but a few.

So despite the Career Advisor's suggestion for Sidney to leave school early and do a TAFE course, Sidney ploughed on. Sidney blitzed his HSC and scooped the pool on awards night for effort, persistence, improvement and contribution to the school and community.

Subsequently, Sidney then did nursing and then decided he could do Medicine. After several successful years as an ED nurse and with some credits from nursing, Sidney enrolled in Medicine!

Sidney is now not only a dad and partner but, very recently, Sidney graduated in Medicine and is currently working as an ED doctor, in Queensland, attending to small things and big things! Sidney has earned the respect of his colleagues as "a bloody good doctor", handling everything from reassuring an injured child or helping save a life, holding a dying patient's hand or managing an ice-afflicted teenager.

Sidney's success is all about self-belief. "If you don't believe in yourself, then you're at the mercy of what everyone else says about you, and that's a mind field."

Sidney's self-belief, grit, determination and persistence allowed him to punch above his weight and burst through that back door into the profession he chose so many years ago.

If you have a child who's struggling, keep in mind Sidney's story. If we can help children find something they're passionate about achieving, we're blooming lucky.

Sidney, I salute you!

Editorial comment:
As a former School Principal, I read this story with particular fascination. How often does the system fail students like Sidney? If not for his positivity, he might have been tragically left behind rather than achieving the impossible.

"A positive thinker sees the invisible, feels the intangible, and achieves the impossible!"
– Winston Churchill

Story 9

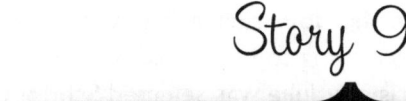

Julie

Julie was worried about her
body shape but decided that she would like
herself anyway

Julie was the sort of friend everyone should have – always looked on the sunny side, cup always half-full rather than half-empty, always able to see a way through a problem.

And she had plenty of problems. Dad was an alcoholic and died young, leaving their mother with five children to run the dairy, bring the Friesian cows in for milking, night and morning, make the butter, stoke up the wood fire stove and all the other work that goes into farm life.

In addition, Julie had to look after her four siblings and yet do her studies. Julie worked hard and was always trying to be the eldest child, the one on whom mum could rely. Unsurprisingly, Julie was selected School Captain, not for being bright but for being a bright thinker.

Julie encouraged her younger sister, Val, to stand up for herself and not be put down by boys trying to pretend they were superior. Val questioned why, at Narrabri Public School, it was only the boys who rang the bell for recess. When Val didn't get any logical answer, one day she raced ahead and rang the bell, albeit five minutes too early, but from then on, the school accepted girls into the bell ringers' club!

As happens when the fickle finger of fate points its digit your way, Julie married, had two boys, and then her husband died. Julie floundered for some years, then got help from a clinical hypnotherapist – so much so that she gave up her retail job and became a very successful clinical hypnotherapist.

Julie piled on the weight until she was embarrassed by her appearance in the mirror. So Julie went to the gym and got a ruthless gym instructor, Grant, who determined that Julie would be his big success story. Then her eldest son died in a car accident and, as you would expect, Julie blamed herself and self-indulgent mothering for the family catastrophe.

The pressure kept mounting on Julie to fulfil Grant's ambition, so she worked, and she worked at it. Eventually, Julie and her new partner Phil decided they needed a break. They went on a cruise, without Grant's approval, just to have a good time.

While Julie was on the cruise at an after-dinner dance, she heard Lesley Gore's song "It's My Party, and I'll Cry if I Want to". She now had her answer to the well-meaning but pushy Grant. When she got home, she invited Grant and his partner around for drinks and then burst into song, "It's my body, and I'll cry if I want to, cry if I want to. You would cry too if it happened to you. "

Grant and the group laughed, but Julie had a big victory. She would no longer be pushed around by what everyone else said she should do. She's still one of Grant's clients, but she's now in charge; it's her body, and she'll cry if she wants to!

Editorial comment:
It's a wonder that Julie wasn't crushed by her experiences. She had such a hard life that reading the story I found myself hoping for a happy ending. I'm pleased I wasn't disappointed.

"Nothing builds self-esteem and self-confidence like accomplishment."
– Thomas Carlyle

Jeannie

Often the most successful adults have had to
rise above childhood setbacks – this famous
lady gives us a lesson in doing it tough

Celebrity Contribution

$\mathcal{I}$ wonder how many of us remember Jeannie Little, the quirky, gifted entertainer with that Australian drawl. Jeannie and her husband Barry had one of the oldest houses in Pearl Beach on the NSW Central Coast, and my family had the other one (but we claim ours was the oldest). Our place was named Noonameena, which means a sleeping place in the bush. Jeannie's was named Shangri-la – Utopia.

As you know, Jeannie passed on not long ago after the all too familiar battle with dementia. But I had massive respect for this lovely lady hiding behind her uneducated image. Jeannie was so kind and time generous that when I was launching my "Who'd Be A Parent" book and I had a lap-sized Sandy as my muppet, she came on TV to support me! I will never forget that, and after the interview, I asked her for her take on parenting as a busy mum. Here's an extract of what she said:

> There have been many hard passages in our parenting, but one I'll always remember was when I was told I had cancer and had to have an operation. The specialist said that he'd have either good news or bad news for me when I woke up. The first thing I remember after the operation was Katie's little school hat bending over my bed, and she said, "Mum, you're going to live after all." I then sank back into sleep, but I'll never forget that moment. It changed my life; I realised that Katie and Barry were all that mattered, and other things in my life would have to fit around them, and I've tried to keep those values ever since.

> We've had some tough financial times. Sometimes we could only afford to eat mince and sausages, but we got by and had a good laugh later. As long as you love each other and talk it out, things will work out. I think too many couples would rather walk out than talk it out, and it's all too easy.

> But don't stay just for the kids. My mum was married to a man who used alcohol too much. It was a miserable life for us all. She asked her parents if she could come back and live there, and they said, "No, you've made your bed; now lie on it." I think that was so heartless, and I don't understand it.

> Later on, when mum had had enough, she packed up all seven of us kids and moved into a little weatherboard house, and we were all really happy even though we were dreadfully poor. Mum started her own

*shop and helped my brothers get started in a wrought iron business.
I remember mum drawing the wrought iron designs on the kitchen
table. But the boys all did very well, and I'll always admire my mum's
courage. Mum didn't complain or sit back and take it; she got up and
did something to make things better.*

*The point I'm trying to make is that not everyone can have two ideal
parents, but if you can have one wonderful parent as I did, that's
enough, don't complain; get out and have a go!*

*When things got me down, I often did what my mother taught me, and
she taught me a lot. She would read tea leaves, sounds silly, but they
always gave me a lift with something good ahead, so things weren't all
bad.*

What common sense, eh! Thinking back over so many years and so many
wonderful people, I realise that very few of my heroes had it easy as kids
– their values, love, faith, and hope were all honed over testing times. Yet,
we often try hard to make it easy for our children and grandkids. Maybe
in trying so hard, we're depriving them of any chance of finding their own
greatness. So perhaps we should rest easy, whatever our failures. These
can well be the springboard to another person's success.

Editorial comment:
*How wonderful to have a neighbour living in Shangri–la! We can't all live
next door to a treasure like Jeannie Little but we can all benefit from the
lessons she learnt in life.*

*"Parents can only give good advice or put them on the right paths, but the
final forming of a person's character lies in their own hands."*
– Anne Frank

Series 2

Phillip

Phillip reverts to white lies to solve his Santa
problems

*D*o you think it's justified to tell a "white" lie? Phillip was guilty of that, but he was a master of quick thinking. I have many of his exploits in mind, but his handling of the Christmas ritual takes the cake.

Talking about rituals reminds me just how important they are to our emotional survival. Just for a moment, think about your habits over birthdays, Easter egg hunts, the Christmas symbols on the tree, the present opening format, your Sunday night dinners etc. Those rituals continue over the generations and in recent times scientists are discovering the strong stabilising role rituals play in our mental health.

One of those rituals in many homes is the Santa visit, where my friend Phillip was a master. His family's ritual for Santa's visit dated back at least three generations, but last year things went wrong. Phillip's family were devout Catholics. Their custom was for the extended family, about 30 in total, to get together at Phillip and Jan's place on Christmas Eve for a big barbecue. Then the group would split up, some off home to bed and some to prepare for Santa, and then some would go off to midnight Mass. That meant each family would wake up Christmas morning, perform their own routines, and celebrate the wonder of wonders in their traditional way. In Phillip and Jan's home, and before the visitors arrived, the kids would help dad get everything set, including the Christmas cake for Santa.

Every year, after the kids had gone to bed and before he went to Mass, it was Phillip's job to eat half of Santa's cake. Last year, things were rushed. The barbecue had been a bit of a culinary disaster. Dad was hassled and, in his haste, forgot to attend to the eating of the cake ritual.

Now keep in mind that their son, Barney, aged seven, thought the sun, moon and stars shone out of dad. But on Christmas morning, the whole fabric of their faith came unstuck big time. The kids had gone out to check that Santa had been and left the presents and there was the cake, untouched!

Barney raced into his parents' bedroom, tears streaming down his face and screaming at dad, "You're a liar. I don't believe you anymore. There's no Santa. We left out the cake for him, and it's still there. I hate you." Barney then ran back into his room, howling his eyes out.

Jan touched Phillip on the arm and whispered, "I think it's about time for you and Barney to have a big talk. He's ready to know the truth." Phillip climbed slowly out of bed and trudged his way into his son's room. He knew this wasn't going to be easy. He entered and shut the door. Ten minutes later, a much happier dad and a much brighter Barney emerged.

"Are you OK, son?" asked his anxious mum.
"Yeah, I'm good, but I wish dad had told me that Santa was on a diet and couldn't eat fruit cake!"

Well done, dad. Welcome to the Storytellers' Club. Sometimes white lies, half-truths, creative compositions are not only forgivable but necessary to add spice to life, build imagination, and offer a distraction from the day-to-day grind of responsibility and chores. Long live laughter and the stress relief that lurks therein.

Editorial comment:
I'm not sure I agree with Dr John's summary of this story. I've seen too many examples where telling a white lie to save the day has led to misery down the track.

"Lies are neither bad nor good. Like a fire, they can either keep you warm or burn you to death; depending on how they're used."
– Max Brooks

Story 12

Alicia

Alicia learns to use less confrontational
techniques to handle her difficult son

If you've been feeling a bit down or had trouble communicating with your kids, spare a thought for Alicia.

Alicia had two teenage boys. The three of them had survived without dad around for ten years. A car accident had landed him in a nursing home with quadriplegia, and all Dave could do was nod, shake, smile, or cry out in pain. Can you imagine what that was like for each of them? And what a life for Alicia, dealing with two testosteroney boys all on her own and then having to support Dave. She couldn't even start a new life. Her older son, Jamie, was a challenging and defiant kid who claimed his quieter brother, Peter, was the favourite. Alicia found it all hard work, but three things got her through – great friends, a different communication style and positive affirmations.

Alicia was lucky to have good friends, but the other changes she made were strictly down to her. She had spent a lot of time yelling at her boys, but she changed this, and the positive affirmations were her daily reference points.

- We do not have to know how to forgive. All we have to do is to be willing to forgive. The universe will take care of the how.
- Every day cannot be good, but there can be good in every day.
- This is a new day. Begin anew to claim and create all that is good.
- If you want love and acceptance from your family, then you must have love and acceptance for them.

Alicia stopped yelling and changed her management style; instead of forcing Jamie's help, she didn't give him any support or privileges unless he pulled his weight.

Instead of yelling, she would leave written messages on Jamie's bed, stated as "I would like", and couched in a few words of love, rather than as an attacking "you" message. Alicia found this took the sting out of the arguments and avoided confrontation. Jamie had to write "I" messages back like, "I feel left out" or, "I hate not being able to have any fun around the house". Mum found it easier to handle that as it was a statement rather than a direct attack and not delivered right in her face.

Alicia saved one of Jamie's "I" messages to show me, "I bet I'm hated so much I won't even get an X-Box like Peter's for Christmas." This dark period in Alicia's life was some years ago now and as is the case for many of our families, you're there for their hard times and then they drift away when they grow beyond needing your help. That's the way it has to be. But I know that Dave passed away some five years ago, and Alicia returned to Brisbane to be closer to her sister. And Jamie, the tear-away, has an IT job and a pad in the inner city. He and his mum, I believe, now get on very well, albeit from a distance.

Kids are hard work, people are hard work. Crises come, but crises go – so just go easy on yourself and try a critical in-look instead of an angry out-look. As the great Civil Rights activist, Martin Luther King, said, "Only when it's dark enough can you see the stars."

Editorial comment:
A wise old teacher taught his less experienced colleagues not to shout at the kids, nor to take their behaviour personally, but to see it as a teaching and learning opportunity. Parents can do the same.

"Kids may not hear us shout at two paces, but they hear our silence a block away."
– Anon

Story 13

Jonno

My colleague gives us all a lesson in
remaining calm under fire

*M*aybe you've got someone in your life who can be just so reassuringly calm in a crisis. My colleague, John, (who I affectionately called Jonno) certainly was that for me. He was always so wise and practical and funny, but there was that other quality to John that emerged often, and I remember one day in particular.

It was a wild and windy day, the sort of day when nature seemed to be venting its spleen, and kids joined in. I had a particular case with a young boy, Joshua, who had Down's Syndrome and was proving a handful for his parents.

They needed to speak to me without Josh, so we set him up in the waiting room with a kids' TV program. I then took the extra precaution of alerting the secretaries that Josh was a somewhat uninhibited boy, and I asked them to ensure that they kept an eye on him and didn't let him break in on our session.

John was in the adjoining room doing a hypnotherapy session with a chap on leave due to dysfunctional anxiety. John told me at the end of the day that his session had gone something like this. He was in the process of getting this chap to relax and focus just on John's voice.

"Damien, I just want you to relax, shut your eyes and listen to my voice. Just leave the outside world behind for a little while and enjoy the peace."

At that point, with the storm raging outside, a branch slapped at the window, and John could see Damien was getting agitated. So, he tried hard to get Damien to ignore it and re-focus on his voice. Having achieved that, a large tree branch hanging over the Clinic fell with a loud thump onto the wrought iron roof. Damien startled and opened his eyes, and gripped the sides of the couch.

Again, John managed to draw him back to their room, and Damien started to relax again. They were just getting back into their session when suddenly their door was flung open and in burst Joshua. He had my soft toy Fuddle, from the WorryWoos kit, clutched under his arm, and he was looking for his parents. My very embarrassed secretary closely followed and swung Josh into her arms and apologised profusely and repeatedly to John and Damien as she took Josh back to the TV. This was all too much for Damien, and now nothing could re-settle him.

At no stage did John raise his voice or lose his secure connection with Damien. But he did apologise to Damien, and they rescheduled their session for after-hours on the same day. So calm under fire. When I asked John how he did it, he said he just did to himself what he was asking Damien to do – breathe deeply and slowly, so the Amygdala didn't hi-jack the brain and panic reigns. The truth is nothing is ever resolved or improved once the Amygdala takes over and we get into fight or flight mode, but sometimes it's hard to stay that calm.

Good on you, Jonno! Don't you just admire people who can do that?

Editorial comment:
Dr John's former colleague was one of those rare souls who could keep calm under pressure. I'm sure many of us wish that we had been blessed with the same gift, but maybe this is something that can be taught as well as caught.

"He who is of calm and happy nature will hardly feel the pressure of age, but to him who is of an opposite disposition, youth and age are equally a burden."
– Plato

Story 14

Bart

Our pet dog Bart takes us
back to our emotional core

ave you ever had a pet that became your Humble Hero? It's not just their friendship, protection, incredible devotion and company – research tells us that when we stroke pets, it seems to earth our emotional electricity, reducing our anger and anxiety. Dogs especially are always so glad to have you home, probably delighted that you're game enough to enter such a mad house – and it's so lovely to come home to a character that wags its tail, not its tongue.

One particular dog made his mark on me forever. He was a scruffy, flea-infested, Cairn terrier the kids found on the beach and carried home. We called him Bart, short for Bartholomew. He just wanted to be with us in the car, down on the sand, on the lounge, anywhere we were.

As time wore on, Bart just wore out. He became incontinent, couldn't climb stairs and went blind. The family decided to have him euthanised. My wife, Jean, insisted that he be cremated, and we still have the urn with his ashes and the photo to go with it. With many tears and last hugs, we took the vet's advice and held Bart as the needle took effect.

As you can imagine, we went through lots of self-doubt and guilt about whether we did the right thing for a long, long time after. However, our brother Alan, another dog lover, sent us this poem. I know not its origin, so I am unable to give due credit. It's called "The Last Battle" and reads this way:

> If it should be that I grow frail and weak
> And pain should keep me from my sleep,
> Then will you do what must be done,
> For this – the last battle – can't be won.
> You will be sad I understand,
> But don't let grief then stay your hand,
> For on this day, more than the rest,
> Your love and friendship must stand the test.
> We have had so many happy years,
> You wouldn't want me to suffer so.
> When the time comes, please, let me go.
> Take me to where to my needs they'll tend.
> Only, stay with me till the end

And hold me firm and speak to me
Until my eyes no longer see.
I know in time you will agree
It is a kindness you do to me.
Although my tail its last has waved,
From pain and suffering I have been saved.
Don't grieve that it must be you
Who has to decide this thing to do;
We've been so close — we two — these years,
Don't let your heart hold any tears.
— Author Unknown

One of our girls put the poem under the photo of Bart with her own little poem she had found that read, "If tears could form a stairway and memories a lane, I'd walk right up to heaven and bring you back again. "

Grieve we did, and probably still do when Bart comes to mind. But tears of grief are very therapeutic and cleansing. As the old Jewish proverb says, "What soap is for the body, tears are for the soul. "

Coincidentally, as we floundered as a family to deal with the loss of our little mate, we were reading a book and this quote just jumped right off the page, "Don't cry because it's over. Smile because it happened. "

Editorial comment:
So many people will be able to relate to this simple but powerful story. As I read Dr John's words, memories of former animal friends from decades ago came sharply into focus in my mind. Humble heroes don't have to be human to leave their mark on your soul.

"Until one has loved an animal, a part of one's soul remains unawakened. "
— Anatole France

Story 15

Rachel

Rachel out-trumps my
scepticism with her worry dolls

You would have loved Rachel. She was the sort of kid who keeps your soul young and puts a skip into your tired step. To be honest, I forget why her parents brought her into the Clinic; probably, they were trying to understand her. But over the years, I've learned that when you're in sessions with young kids, you've got to engage their sense of fun, play, and imagination, or the relationship just doesn't click.

I've yet to be asked to treat any adolescent or adult with a Santa fixation or Easter Bunny or Tooth Fairy obsession. Still, I've had to treat thousands who have lost their sense of fun and fantasy and can't imagine anything good happening in their lives.

In the Clinic, I had my few magic tricks and unique gemstones with "special powers". I'd have special dolls with powers to chase away any night-time monsters, or if they wanted religious reassurance, I might use the power of the cross.

But Rachel caught me out at my own game. She was convinced that her little worry dolls could beat every problem. When I challenged her, Rachel said she would prove it to me. She reached into her little handbag and pulled out a few of the "worry dolls" her parents had bought at a Bali street stall. Rachel asked me to choose anyone I liked. I picked one we called Tanika and put it on my desk, standing upright in a little blob of Blu Tak.

Rachel promised that if I kept Tanika with me, nothing terrible would happen. But without a word of a lie, I had a car run into the back of my new car between that appointment and her follow-up visit. I lost my wallet and misplaced my car keys. At our next meeting, as I handed Tanika back to her, I told Rachel of my depressing news since being "blessed" with Tanika!

She looked at me wide-eyed and said, "Well, did you find your car keys?" I told her I hadn't, but we did get new keys cut.

"Did you find your wallet?" I mumbled that I had eventually found it, shoved under the side of the car seat.

"And", she went on, "Have you fixed your car smash?" When I reluctantly confessed that the other driver had to pay, Rachel threw up her arms in evidence. "I told you everything would work out if you let Tanika look after you, and she has!"

I was lost for words, once again gob-smacked by the incredible faith of a young child. No doubt Rachel has put away all those childish things now she is a grown-up. But I do know we're all better off with faith and hope and love in our lives. And if I'm honest, I hope Rachel still has MY Tanika somewhere close by to remind her that our worries come to pass!

Long live Tanika. I suppose the other good news is that, regardless of what the mirror might say, within our souls, we are never too old to enjoy our childhood!

Editorial comment:
I hope Dr John has read Dr Norman Swan's latest book, "So You Want To Live Younger Longer?" It might just help him die young as late as possible.

"Three things will last forever: faith, hope, and love — and the greatest of these is love."
— Corinthians 1, Chapter 13:13

Story 16

Brian

A wonderful little story about some
forensic psychology to handle problems

$\mathcal{M}$aybe you've got a kid somewhere in your life who impressed you in some quirky way.

For me, that was young Brian. His mum brought him into the Clinic because he had developed these scary panic attacks and nightmares about dad, with whom he'd always got on well! Just mentioning dad's name would set Brian off, and he would shake, squirm, develop sweaty palms and have trouble breathing.

At night, Brian would go to bed quite happily and then wake just before midnight screaming. Mum would race in to find Brian in the foetal position at the top of the bed, stuttering and stammering and trying to say he'd just seen dad standing in the doorway looking at him.

When Brian was asked why he had become so scared of dad, he'd get quite agitated and blurt out, "Cause he hit me really hard." It turns out that three years earlier, dad had spanked him for throwing a stone at a car!

But now, this is where Brian was something special. He became very forensically interested in why it should come back to haunt him three years after the stone-throwing incident when it hadn't been a problem till now.

With mum's help, we dug deeper. Brian's parents had separated not long back, so could that be the reason? Was he attempting to get his dad back? "No," said Brian, "If I wanted dad back, I wouldn't have awful nightmares about him, would I?" But mum said she was very upset when dad had spanked Brian for the stone-throwing AND she had been very upset when they separated!

Brian and I came to think there could be a link because mum had yelled at dad to get out, and Brian could remember her saying, "Get out and never darken these doors again." Now, that may be a common thing for an adult to say but a weird thing for a child to hear. In the black-and-white mind of a primary school-aged child the world has goodies and baddies, and as mum was a goody, dad had to be the baddy.

So, Brian and I worked out that if dad was the baddy, all the love he had for dad had to be turned upside down to hate, and the only thing he could remember to hate was the spanking he got over that stone-throwing. All the hugs, bike rides, and wrestles he enjoyed with his dad were pushed right out of his thinking, and he focused hard on his hate. Brian had now conjured up an image of dad as an ogre that preyed on him day and night.

Once Brian could grasp how his mind had been playing tricks on him, normal remedial methods could work. We gradually started some desensitisation, starting with taking a phone call from dad, to meeting with mum and dad at the Coffee Club for a smoothie, to going surfing just with dad. We were over the hump, and their love did the rest!

Their relationship headed north in a hurry with a cooperative mum, a forensically talented son and a patient dad. I haven't seen them for a while, but now he's a teenager I'd imagine that his room would be such a pigsty — no intruder, let alone dad, could get through his doorway anyhow.

Good kids and loving families go through tough times, but they come out the other end! To keep the image rolling, with "faith, hope and charity", you can bet that better times are just through that doorway!

Editorial comment:
This story reminded me of Wordsworth's "Prelude" where he muses about the confusing images seen beneath the surface, in the river from a boat. Brian's story is a lesson in looking beneath the surface to discover the real issues when we don't understand other people or how they are behaving.

"As one who hangs, down-bending from the side
Of a slow-moving boat, upon the breast
Of a still water, solacing himself
With such discoveries as his eye can make...
Yet often is perplex'd, and cannot part
The shadow from the substance, rocks and sky."

Story 17

Craig

Craig uses his art to share his pain,
and mum and dad learn a big lesson
in cooperation

What would be your best way of handling emotional stress? Some talk it out, some run it out, some play it out, some hug it out, some act it out, and artistic folk draw it out.

Let me tell you about Craig and his art. Craig was a mess — teary, testy, tight tummies and very angry. His parents had separated three years earlier and Craig missed dad big time. dad said he missed Craig and his brother heaps, but it was all mum's fault, so that put Craig into a spin. Does he believe his mum or his dad?

The problem doubled this year when dad teamed up with another lady, Cherise, and he became a distracted dad. When it was access weekend dad and the boys now spent the weekend at Grandma's. If the kids phoned dad midweek, often the call would end up in a tirade from dad against mum.

When dad was due to pick up the boys for the weekend, he was often late because he had to pick Cherise up after work.

The crisis came last holidays when dad was due to take the boys away, but Cherise had other plans, and she called off the week.

However, this story has a fascinating twist. I was making videos about the "Worrywoos" at a local school with teachers telling us how they used and adapted the little monsters.

One teacher with the older children said she had the class create their own monsters. It turns out that Craig was in that group and had created a new monster, "Pullo", drawn with two heads — to show kids torn between mum and dad! How clever was that!

When I got to chat with Craig about Pullo he teared up, so we looked at the problem through dad's eyes. He, too, was torn between his kids and Cherise.

But Sandy, his mum, also heard about Craig's Pullo and decided enough was enough. Through her friends, Sandy gained the confidence to say that word we all hate but sometimes need: NO!

Sandy still took the line that dad loved the boys, but there'd be no more what she called "do-si-doing" around dad. Now the family went on with their life and dad would have to fit in. If dad was way late for access, Sandy would go on with whatever she was doing and leave a message on the door explaining where to pick up the boys. And there'd be no more upsetting and frustrating calls to dad unless there was something fantastic to tell. Dad could call them.

To Craig's surprise (and delight), dad lifted his game. He now calls twice a week, is always on time for his weekend pick-up, and I'll bet next holidays won't be a problem (at least for the kids). Craig's tight tummies have disappeared, and he's performing much better at home and school. Well done, Pullo!

Editorial comment:
Sometimes I think we rely too much on people "talking" out their pain. Some can't and don't function that way. Maybe we could all learn a lesson from Craig and his drawing. For millennia, people have relied on the arts for communication, self-expression and therapy.

"Art is you being free from all of the world's heaviness."
– Unknown

Joanne

Joanne may have only lived
briefly but she taught us all so much

Isn't it funny that some people you can know for a lifetime and not think about them, and others come into your life briefly but leave a huge legacy?

Joanne was like that. I got to know her at the Clinic. Her parents brought her in with her five-year-old brother, Troy, for grief counselling – not for Joanne or her brother but for their mum and dad. I recall her as a bright-eyed girl of about eight who quickly won over the hearts of all the staff.

Joanne had a particularly debilitating form of that horrid lung disease, cystic fibrosis (CF) – and the prognosis was not good. So, as those of you who have had anything to do with CF will know, there was the constant surveillance, the fear of germs, the massaging, the coughing and frequent visits to the hospital and specialists. But Joanne had a joy in her step and soul that inspired all of us who had the privilege to know her. I say "had that privilege" because Joanne died a while back. But her school and friends have all been changed by her short life.

What impressed everyone was that death didn't scare Joanne, even though it scared her friends. So, after her death, they asked their teacher lots of questions like, "How can she get to Heaven if she's buried under the ground?"

The teacher listened, and they shared their grieving, and that helped. Then they talked about why they admired Joanne and I think, there's much we can learn from their comments.

> "Joanne enjoyed each day and didn't fret
> over yesterday or worry about tomorrow."
> "She never bore grudges."
> "Joanne trusted people, and poor
> though her health may have been, she was rich in her love."
> "She never got bogged down in nasty
> things about people. Life was too short for that."

The kids decided that Joanne may be dead but her messages would live on in their hearts forever. They put flowers on her desk for some time, then used an artificial flower arrangement when the flowers wilted. They left her seat vacant for the rest of the year.

But Joanne proved a point we all know but forget. Our riches are not in how long we've lived but in how we've lived!

It's odd, but some people can be so scared of death that they live life so poorly and kids like Joanne can live so briefly yet leave everyone richer.

Editorial comment:
As a school principal, I shared a family's pain as they experienced the loss of not one child but two to cystic fibrosis. Those good people learnt all about living life to the full in the face of terrible adversity. Our riches are not in how long we've lived but in how we've lived.

"When the one great scorer comes to mark against your name, He writes not that you won or lost, but how you played the game."
– Grantland Rice

Story 19

Scott

Radio personality Scott gives me a huge
lesson in multi-tracking and multi-tasking

*H*ave you noticed that, as you get older, your mind and body face their D-day? They either decline, droop, drop, dry or dribble.

But it's our mind's decline that I find most perplexing. Whereas in our younger years we could juggle three or four thoughts simultaneously without losing track, now, as we age, our minds can't multi-track but just work on dichotomies – we can think about this or that, but not together. Men seem particularly prone to this D-Day decline. We go off to do one thing, another thought crosses our mind. We go off to do that and forget what we were going to do in the first place.

One man who bucked that trend was our local ABC radio announcer Scott. I've known Scott for over thirty years on various radio stations around the country, so I well and truly know his style. Considering that the country's best and busiest TV and radio personalities have interviewed me over the years, Scott stands out as the most dynamic I have ever met!

I was a regular on his program for many years, discussing some aspects of Family Psychology. The night before my Friday guest spot, I would send the topic, background and a few questions for Scott to ask me so he didn't have to do any other background research. I'm not sure many of you know the set-up of a radio station. Anyway, I would be sitting in the studio opposite Scott, with the colossal sound console between us, and the producer's window and control room behind me over my right shoulder. The producer would do our sound level checks while Scott would be doing the traffic or weather report. Then he would turn to me – but that's when the mind boggling, multi-tracking mix of messages began!

My topic could be, say, "Helping Kids to Concentrate" with the aim of helping them to avoid distractions, and what would Scott do? He'd be having a field day with the producer behind me – pointing, scowling, shaking his head, mouthing words, pretending to slit his throat, checking traffic, and checking news feeds. All the while, I was expected to concentrate on concentration – keep my thoughts focused, sequenced, and articulate, and at the same time, the Station expected me to keep our listeners riveted to the topic.

When I paused for breath, Scott would chime in with an incredibly pertinent question, probably not one on my list, but absolutely spot-on.

Scott was always courteous, always on the ball, and never lost focus on the topic or what I was saying, even though he was processing hundreds of mixed messages. How Scott did that I will never know. He certainly tested my capacity to concentrate! But this incredible man turned this personal propensity into a public positive.

Scott was much more than that. Scott helped every charity he could – sporting, cultural, musical, performing arts, indigenous issue, disability you name it. There was no ego in it – Scott went out of his way to support local enterprises because he could!

Maybe you have someone in your life like Scott, who turned his hyperactive multi-tracking into some creative magic. The lesson I got from Scott and so many other clients over the years seems that so often, it's the ones who rise above their challenges who have the most to offer.

Some time ago, they asked me if I would put a letter of support in for Scott for the Australia Day awards, but I can do better than that. I proudly welcome Scott into the Humble Heroes' Hall of Fame for his intellect, oral memory, and sheer capacity to multi-track and multi-serve.

Editorial comment:
Towards the end of my career, I was privileged to be awarded an OAM. At the same time a former student of mine was also awarded an OAM for sporting excellence despite having cerebral palsy. His award made me feel like an impostor. I was just doing my job. He was overcoming adversity and excelling at the highest level.

"I love my disability. It is the best thing that ever happened to me. It really is, and I'm so thankful for the life that I get to live."
– Dylan Alcott

Story 20

Bryce

Famous writer Bryce Courtenay, in "April Fool's
Day", wrestles with lessons learnt at his
son's bedside

Celebrity Contribution

*I*f you had the chance to meet someone famous who had made a significant impact on you or whom you admired, would you be able to reel off a few names?

One such character for me was Bryce Courtenay, the famous author of so many books, including, for my purposes here, his tell-tale book "April Fool's Day". When we met in the Green Room, waiting to be called into the TV studio, I asked Bryce if he'd like to make a guest's contribution to my "Who'd Be a Parent" book. A week later, I got a note from him, which I've always treasured. Here is a heavily condensed excerpt.

> *Dear Dr John, I don't know what you'd like to know about my story. I do know that being a parent is, without any doubt, the greatest challenge I have ever faced. As you know, we reared three boys (which is a challenge in itself) but Damon, our youngest, was a haemophiliac with medically acquired AIDS, who died at the age of 24. Maybe the best I can offer has been said in "April Fool's Day", which is Damon's book. Maybe some of my early recollections of the long lonely hours of parenting a sick child will strike a chord in those parents who've been through something similar.*
>
> *Throughout his life Damon was to have at least three blood transfusions a week and sometimes more. We would put him to bed at night not knowing how long it would be before we were wakened to his cry. Later, when he could walk, he would come to my bedside and tug on my arm, "Wake up daddy, I've got another bleed."*
>
> *It was always my job to wake up at night and attend to Damon. I'd flop into bed exhausted only to be awakened two hours later by a Damon tug on my arm. Sometimes my head would be splitting and my mouth tasting like the inside of a parrot's cage. I often found this hard and felt sorry for myself.*
>
> *Even so, there is something that happens to you when you have a critically ill child. Damon's haemophilia called for an emotional neutrality. We decided it must never interfere with the opportunities available to Brett and Adam. They must not feel its impact on their lives. And so you couldn't in the end allow yourself to react emotionally to the circumstances around you, his bleeds and the procedure they involved took precedence over everything else. When you were in the Damon box, the haemophilia compartment –*

*you simply got on with things and tried to create as little fuss as possible.
There was an emotional price to pay for this – sometimes I appear very
cold and unfeeling. However the discipline involved in conducting one's life in
this way is not good for the human soul.*

*Looking back, those long nights were my real time with Damon, the time
a father should spend with his sons, but never really allows time for in
everyday life. Damon and I grew up together in the dark hours when most
of the world and almost all the kids in it, were asleep.*
April Fool's Day. P 48.

Fathers are you listening? Did I? Would I? And I wonder what impact such
skewed parenting had on his marital relationship? I can't ask him now of
course.

Editorial comment:
*Dr John has met many ordinary people in his career and some
extraordinary folk as well. I love the lessons we can all draw from Dr
John's encounter with one of our most famous and prolific novelists.*

*"Negativity is an addiction to the bleak shadow that lingers around
every human form – you can transfigure negativity by turning it toward
the light of your soul."*
– John O'Donohue

Series 3

Story 21

With creative thinking,
AJ's family learns how to handle his ADHD

This story has a dubious moral, but young AJ and his family cemented a place in my heart, so I feel compelled to share it.

If you've never had or lived with a child with ADHD or ADD, you're entitled to be sceptical and blame bad parenting. But, if you've got a child with this disorder, then maybe you'll get a chuckle out of dad's efforts to help AJ find his place in life and give you some food for thought from mum's contribution.

AJ had all the classic symptoms – fidgety, poor listener, couldn't sit still, easily distracted, disruptive, never finished anything, and, as you'd expect, was driving his parents insane. He came from a great home with very involved parents, and their other two kids were relatively "normal". We tried behavioural tactics such as strict rules, regular routines, rehearsing desired behaviours, and using water, music, and trampolining to soothe his system. Then we checked food intolerances and found that AJ had several, but red colouring was his worst. Still, his parents felt like the greatest failures in parentdom. Then we organised a trial on psychostimulant medication, and that worked wonders.

AJ became a different boy. He improved in behaviour, schoolwork and self-esteem, but football was the only exercise he yearned for, so dad sponsored the local footy team. That way, because he was the sponsor, he had a hand in team selection and got AJ on the team as a fumbly forward.

Unfortunately, AJ was measured and thoughtful while on his medication but had no flair. When they took him off his medication at weekends, as many parents do, he was back to his old active bustly self and ran, chased, tackled and played much better. The coach also noticed the difference, even more so when AJ added a red toffee apple to his pregame preparation, so he put the whole team on red cordial at halftime, and they cleaned up the comp! True story.

Mum felt a bit excluded from this boy's club, but she was a great mum and brought me this poem, which she asked me to share with other families trying to cope with a child like AJ.

Have you ever seen the turmoil a single child can cause?
From sunrise until sunset, he can go without a pause.
He drives his parents crazy, his teachers up a tree,
But he can't really help this, 'cause he has ADD.

Some doctors and some friends of mine, some teachers – so I'm told,
Who don't know what ADD is, and think the child is bold!
They talk about his parents and say they are to blame
But his parents have other children who just are not the same.

The child who is so loving, so trusting, and so kind,
But people who don't understand – they say I must be blind.
And when I try explaining, they tell me to "get real",
Not thinking for one moment, just how this child must feel!

This child has constant turmoil going 'round inside his brain,
He looks at other children and knows he's not the same.
And it's up to us, as people, at school as well as home,
To make sure that this friendless child does not feel all alone.
The moral of this story, and I'm sure you'll all agree,
Is, remember, but for the grace of God, this could be you or me!
- The ADD Child Poem. Pat Ryan. 1997

I'm not sure who deserves the Humble Heroes' Award – AJ for defying labels, dad for hands-on support or mum for everything else and for helping AJ believe in himself. This time I've decided to give the Humble Heroes' Award to the whole family! Well done, team!

Editorial comment:
Parents have a huge role in assisting teachers and others with the care of their ADD children. Collaboration and open communication between parents and teachers is the key. Parents need the teacher's support and may also be able to inform teachers of what works best for their child.

"The hardest thing about ADHD is that it's 'invisible' to outsiders. People just assume that we are not being good parents and that our child is a brat, when they don't have any idea how exhausted we truly are."
– S.C.

Story 22

Winnie

A beautiful story from a grateful nephew in
praise of his beloved Aunt Winnie

Podcast Listener's Humble Hero

*M*aybe you're aware that I put my stories on Spotify in the hope that I could give listeners the opportunity to celebrate and salute their own Humble Heroes. Not long ago, I received this email from Gus.

Dr John, you've asked listeners for their Humble Hero, and I need to tell you about my hero, Aunty Winnie. I'm 73 years old now, but every time I think of special people in my life, I keep returning to my incredible Aunty Winnie.

Going right back to my toddler years, this incredible lady nursed my frail single-parent mother, looked after me and my sister (as well as her own healthy but selfish son), and also her daughter Lorraine who had severe cerebral palsy and suffered daily epileptic seizures – and our Winnie did this all on her own.

That wasn't easy financially either, so Winnie then took in boarders to help make ends meet, taught Sunday School, and cooked meals for the aged and infirm in our country town. Then Winnie had to move back to Sydney to care for her frail dad and dementing mother. When they died, my mum worked six days a week to keep a roof over our head, so Winnie moved back again and became our carer.

With Winnie's help, we survived; we finished school on the Central Coast, and after many wayward years, I settled down and became a builder. But I could never get over Winnie's incredible sacrifices to get me through. As soon as I could afford it, I built a new pair of units, one for my family and one for Winnie. Then her daughter died, and Winnie deteriorated, so it was our turn to look after her.

Her selfish son turned up one day, took over her home and finances, limited the number of visitors, including me, "cleaned" out her cupboards and had a garage sale of her life! Her deterioration accelerated, and I think her heart broke. Winnie was put into the hospital, and her son blithely went home to his family.

That was the beginning of the end for Winnie, but I just have to share the final moments of my Humble Hero. Not too long ago, I sat with Winnie and held her hand as she died, and this lady, the bravest, most generous, uncomplaining, honest, loving and caring person I had ever known, looked across at me, smiled and thanked ME for all I had done.

I swear the staircase would have been lit, and the angels singing as she ascended, and St. Peter would have welcomed her as this humblest of heroes passed through the gates. Vale Winnie.

Editorial comment:
Many years ago, I was living in a remote part of PNG, and the only reading material was an old moth-eaten set of the Complete Works of Charles Dickens. I read the whole bunch. Dickens admired those who practised selfless love but condemned those who sought to further themselves at the expense of others. I was much taken with the realisation that many of his characters exemplify selfless love over selfishness. Consider, if you will, Nicholas Nickleby, Lucie Manette, Bob Cratchitt and Cissy Jupe.

"I would ask you, dearest, to be very generous with him always, and very lenient on his faults when he is not by. I would ask you to believe that he has a heart he very, very seldom reveals."
– Charles Dickens, "A Tale of Two Cities"

Story 23

John

John, of Wayside Chapel fame, writes in with a
wonderful success story about Allan

Podcast Listener's Humble Hero

*I*n my Spotify podcasts, my grandson, Jensen, the editor, would throw open the option of people writing in with their Humble Hero. This story came in from John, a Care Coordinator in the Community Services Centre at Wayside Chapel in Sydney for ten years. Here is his Humble Hero.

Together with the frontline team, we help provide a safe space, vital essentials (such as emergency clothing and showers) and practical support to anyone who walks through Wayside's doors.

Every day, I meet people sleeping rough, in crisis or struggling to cope with the impacts of isolation and rejection. They each have their unique story, and I am here to listen to every one of them – it's one of my favourite parts about this job!

One friendly face I have had the pleasure of meeting is Allan. Allan first came to Wayside at just 14 years old.

Struggling with the loss of his mother, Allan left home because it wasn't safe anymore. He heard about Wayside from someone he met on the streets and decided to check it out. Here was a place where Allan, for the first time, could feel safe and welcome. We helped him secure accommodation and provided necessities to get him back on his feet. Best of all, he was surrounded by a community that encouraged him to celebrate and explore his talents. Wayside was a chance for Allan to start piecing his life back together.

Over the years, I have watched Allan grow from a scared teenage boy to a confident young man with a passion for singing. Music was a way for Allan to stay focused and off the streets. Just recently, Allan wrote his first song and produced his own music video – I'm so proud of him.

Dr John, miracles like this are part and parcel of our day. It's satisfying work, but it's only through public donations that we can go on helping people like Allan on their healing journey. Would you please share this story?

I'm only too honoured to do so.

As Kathy Calvin, CEO and President of the United Nations Foundation, put it, "Giving is not just about making a donation. It is about making a difference."

Story 24

Rob & Carolyn

A wonderful story about sacrificial love
that makes a huge impression on me

Sometimes I get a lesson in selfless love that shakes me to the core. This was the first case I thought of when I was asked to salute all the Humble Heroes in my many years working with families.

Carolyn and Rob were loving grandparents. They came to see me with their daughter Samantha and their gorgeous six-year-old granddaughter, Heidi. Both lived with them since Samantha couldn't cope on her own. As Samantha wanted to talk to me alone, Rob and Carolyn took Heidi into the waiting room.

Through buckets of tears, Samantha told me she had a terminal condition and only had months to live. She asked me to promise I would fight to let Heidi stay with the grandparents when she died. Samantha was extremely angry with her ex, Trent, Heidi's father, who was in the military and living interstate. Samantha claimed Trent had shown scant regard for her feelings or her medical condition, or Heidi.

Of course, I agreed, and six months later, Samantha passed away. Then, as Samantha had predicted, the battle began. Trent said he was next of kin, had a new partner and wanted Heidi to live with him. Trent had taken the matter to court and had a ruling in his favour. So Rob and Carolyn were back to see me, perplexed about what to do, given their enormous love for Heidi and their promise to Samantha to keep Heidi in their care.

As their legal advice was consistent with the court ruling, we decided to forge a link with Trent. Fortunately, he agreed to an amicable staged transfer of Heidi to his care. I'd like to think it was because he trusted me. It started with regular phone calls to Heidi, coming up to see her and taking her out for a fun time together, visiting her school and meeting her friends, then the big trip with Rob and Carolyn to visit dad and meet his partner, Karlye.

Heidi and I had many sessions together — at first, it was sharing her anger, and then, as we progressed, we started to look at the upcoming adventure. Squeek, my Worrywoo plush toy, had been scared to try anything new or take on new adventures, and Heidi needed some grit. To help Heidi, I armed her with the accompanying Andi Green book, "The Monster in the Bubble".

That process took about nine months, and Trent issued his ultimatum; he wanted Heidi to start the New Year living with them and attending their local school.

This all happened about four years ago; Heidi is settled in her new home, has a great group of close friends and has taken up cheerleading. She rings Carolyn about once a week, and they have been down to see her in her new life.

So the outcome is all good, I suppose. I sometimes see Rob at the hardware store where he works part-time, and it's all amicable. "How is Carolyn?" I ask. He replies, "She's OK, she still aches for Heidi and her daughter." "How are you, Rob?" His eyes well up, and he just says, "OK."

Would I do anything differently if I had the case again? I don't think so. It was for the best, as per the court decree. But it did remind me of two big lessons. The first is just how adaptable children are – remember that they are the most adaptable creatures on the planet, bar none – so we probably need to remember that, for the most part, they will adapt, and we don't need to sweat the small stuff. The other lesson is just how awesome was/is that selfless love of Rob and Carolyn! Let's be grateful for the love in our lives – imperfect and indefinite as that may be!
What a lesson, what love – now my eyes are welling up, and I think I'd best leave it there. I just hope Squeek is still doing his job for Heidi.

Editorial comment:
Dr John comments in this story about the adaptability of children. Adaptability, of course, can be learnt, and in my years as a school principal, I became fascinated for a while with the work of Maria Montessori. Adaptability and self-direction are both cornerstones of the Montessori approach to pedagogy.

"Our care of the child should be governed, not by the desire to make him (sic) learn things, but by the endeavour always to keep burning within him that light which is called intelligence."
– Maria Montessori

Story 25

Stan

A rollickingly funny story about my mate Stan
and his incredibly effective methods to achieve
reparations

*Y*ou probably have someone like Stan in your life. He's my Humble Hero for today, perhaps because, in his shy way, he had a unique way of resolving a problem. Stan and I were fellow travellers for some years when we were lecturers in Armidale. We both taught in the Education Department, did Honours together, and won a University Medal. But I was more the extrovert, and Stan was more the introvert. Stan never sought praise or glory and was happy reading, reflecting and very happy in his own company.

Stan displayed his unique problem-solving style after my son, Timmy, was born. Jean and Timmy were both still in the hospital as the specialists assessed his developmental problems. The diagnosis was Down's Syndrome, and the prognosis was not good as Timmy also had a hole in his heart. So I was home alone and quite melancholy, and what can a friend say or do when, like Stan, he didn't have kids himself and wasn't a grief counsellor.

That didn't daunt our Stan one iota. He just rocked up to the door to give me company and brought fish and chips wrapped up in newspaper and a bottle of 1971 Grange! The meal would have cost about $2. 50, and the wine close to 10 times that. I burst out laughing at the sheer incongruity of it all – and Stan just smiled sheepishly. It certainly lifted my spirits.

But that social downplay was not "affected", and Stan infected many colleagues and students in the same way. After he met Noela, Stan decided it was time to become a man of property, so they moved out of town and bought a small farm with a very stately and historic homestead, which they named Gadshill, from Shakespeare's "Henry IV". One of its key attractions to Stan and me was a vast basalt rock cellar where Stan could keep his outstanding collection of vintage wines.

The only problem with this purchase was that this was a farm, and Stan wasn't a farmer! But he knew when on a farm, do what farmers do! Stan bought all the accoutrements. Then his neighbours advised him to buy a few head of cattle to keep the grass down and make the odd bob. When Stan asked how to do that, his neighbours offered to buy the cattle for him and have them trucked in.

Then the problems started; the farm was run down, and Stan's cattle kept breaking through the fences to the neighbours' properties. Hot under the collar, three neighbours fronted Stan about this break-out. Stan apologised sincerely but keeping in mind that Stan was as useless as "teats on a bull" as his neighbours described him, he didn't know what to do about it. So after hearing their complaint, Stan invited them to his cellar to chat and find a way forward. Down they went and some hours later came out with many handshakes and a plan.

The upshot was that Stan bought the wire and his neighbours did the repairs – the farmers were happy, the cattle were happy, and Stan was exceedingly grateful. Of course, when the job was over, they all got back together and toasted each other in Stan's beautiful basalt cellar. That's what I call great diplomacy – using your talents – and this was an incredible display of reparations. If only we could look at every problem as an opportunity for a win-win like Stan achieved, I'm sure the world would be happier.

Stan, I warmly welcome you into the Humble Heroes' Hall of Fame for sheer brilliance in using your strengths to cover your weaknesses.

Editorial comment:
What a character! Stan's experiences tell us that it makes sense to develop our strengths rather than focus on our perceived weaknesses. US researcher Carol Dweck argues that we can improve both strengths and weaknesses.

"People with a growth mindset tend to achieve more than those with a fixed mindset because they put more energy into learning."
– Carol Dweck

Story 26

Dr Tony

Dr Tony changes the course of a boy's
life with a kayak and a bit of caring

Chris would have been about 13 when I first met him. He wasn't in trouble at school but just very flat and non-involved. It was hard for me to get on Chris's wavelength because he just tended to mumble and shrug. Chris didn't have a dad around and never saw his mum, who had a drug problem. He didn't even have much to do with Grandma, who lived alone. Grandma was too busy working and didn't see Chris as her problem. No, Chris lived with his Great Grandma. Joan was in her late 80s, tiny and stooped with a neck brace that seemed to keep her upright. Chris towered over her, but when she said jump, he'd do that.

Chris and Joan lived in a little shack near the water, and Chris loved everything aquatic – fishing, surfing, boating, swimming. As you might gather, Joan was too old and tired for the job life had called her to do. Chris was lost and lonely but knew Granny, as he called her, loved him and wanted the best.

Joan was talking to Dr Tony, her GP, about her boy and lamenting that she just didn't have the energy or resources to keep up with Chris. As it happened, Dr Tony helped run the local troop that the Sea Scouts had started in the bay; his son was a keen member. Dr Tony asked Joan if he could pick up Chris and take him to the Wednesday afternoon Sea Scouts get together. Joan was, of course, delighted. The pick-up and transport happened, and Chris became almost enthusiastic about this venture – even a grin sometimes furtively flashed across his face.

Dr Tony bought Chris his kayak and trailer, with Joan's permission, so he could go fishing and exploring in the bay. Chris was stoked to get his own anything and became a knowledgeable fisherman – keen to learn all the different names of fish types and other aquatic creatures. Since then, we've managed to get Chris in one afternoon a week as a volunteer at the local aquatic display centre.

Last I heard, Chris was still in the Sea Scouts, going to school and living with Granny, who now gets much more in-home support. What lies ahead? Who knows, but Chris has set his sails much straighter now, and he stands taller and brighter. There won't be any public acclaim for Dr Tony, and there won't be any Australia Day awards for Joan. Still, I learnt a lot of respect for frail Joan and mighty appreciation for Dr Tony, who, no doubt, breached professional ethics in stepping in as he did – but when you can make a difference for good, it's a very satisfying feeling.

I think Dr Tony, no matter how many problem patients he had had that day, would breathe deeply and warmly when he thought about this kayak kid, Chris! To all the givers who don't count the cost, I hope you sleep well. The world is a better place for your sacrifice.

Editorial comment:
A joyous and rewarding part of my time as a school principal was visiting our sister schools in other parts of the world. I was fortunate to be able to do this and doubly blessed to be able to visit Glenstal Abbey in Ireland – home to not only a school but a Benedictine Abbey. I was welcomed there with open arms. The Benedictines are famous for their hospitality and we could all take a leaf out of their book (in this case the Rule of St Benedict) and extend friendship and generosity to others without any expectation that they have a favour to return.

The Principal

The Principal wins over staff and students with the motto "This is a no put-down school"

In one of my podcasts, I asked the listeners these questions. Did you go to a good school? Did your kids go to a good school? What made it good or not so good? If you think you went to a good one, maybe write in and tell me what you think makes the difference.

When you think back, you probably remember the teachers you loved or loathed, plays you put on, places you went, friends you made, and bullies you feared, but probably not many would nominate their Principal! Some years ago, I had family reasons to visit this PUBLIC school inter-state, and I was gob-smacked. The kids were being so nice to each other. The interactions between staff and parents were of the same order. When I talked to random kids in the playground, they all said they were going to the best school.

What made this school, which I'll call Positive Public, different? It was a new school amalgamating families from all over the place that had moved into this new lower middle-class estate with some social housing — hardly the formula for an easy school. Many of the "clientele" came with histories of behaviour problems in other schools.

But there were a few features that might have made the difference: they chose the teachers on merit to best use the gifts and talents they thought they could bring to the kids' education, and the Principal was hand selected!

Like every other school, Positive Public had its mission statement and governing ethos. Still, of all the differences, the parents mentioned that the school had decided to adopt one crucial principle — NO PUT-DOWNS! That statement was not restricted to comments from kids to other kids. It meant no put-downs by teachers of children or other teachers, parents or administration staff, and vice versa. It was such a simple statement, but what an impact it made.

At first, the kids thought this was too weird to be true and walked around all day saying, "that's a put-down", "that's a put-down", but as the novelty wore off and the kids saw the teachers meant it and carried it out in their behaviour, things started to change. The number of bullying episodes has dropped to the point of being a non-issue, morale is high, absenteeism of teachers and pupils is way below the State average, and there's an element of fun that you don't often feel in schools.

And there was one other element that had the kids hooked into school – whatever techniques the Principal was using, he had the parents working with him, not against him, and I believe kids felt the force and security of home and school in partnership.

Maybe you think school should mirror life and that put-downs and bullying are part of their learning. The school believes that it has to let kids see that there is another way to interact. A way that does work, and there's plenty of opportunity to tackle that tougher side of life after school, in sport, clubs, at home, with siblings etc.

I think I'm inclined to agree with them. But the proof of the pudding is in the eating – every teacher wants to stay on, and they've got more kids clambering to come in than they can handle. So maybe this Principal got it right – perhaps we're all aching to be part of that school of life where people treat each other with that same respect.

What excellent grooming for happy adults in the future. Well done to that Principal – you're my Humble Hero for today. I wish I'd gone to your school.

Editorial comment:
My school never had such an explicit rule as "no put-downs". Maybe we should have had one. It's not just the children who need to be aware of put-downs but adults too. Some teachers use sarcastic humour and become very defensive when challenged.
Oscar Wilde famously said, "Sarcasm is the lowest form of wit but the highest form of intelligence."

By contrast, a famous US etiquette expert said,
"As a possession for either man or woman, a ready smile is more valuable in life than a ready wit."
– Emily Post

Story 28

Narelle

When life was falling apart for Narelle and she
wanted a nervous breakdown, she found a poem
to help her through

Sharyn handed me this clipping from an article I wrote in the Brisbane News in 1997. She had kept it on her fridge to read when needed. Sharyn found it helpful, so I thought you might too.

To say that Narelle was having a bad hair day underplays what she was experiencing. It wasn't just a bad day. It was an overwhelming series of heartbreaking setbacks. Her husband had left for greener pastures, and her two girls under five were at war, probably because they could sense the anger in the air. To cap it all off, her washing machine had broken down, and while she was trying to get someone to fix it, her preschoolers had drawn with crayons all over the wallpaper in their room.

I don't know what you'd do in this crisis — some cry it out, some try their deep breathing to stay in control, some I know keep a little bag of keepsakes from the kids to remind them that they're not all bad, some will pound their pillow, some will try phoning a friend or anyone who will listen, some will shut the door and suck in fresh air until they can regain their composure, some will scream out to the Almighty to fix it — whatever can get it up and out and hurt nobody else.

Narelle was beyond all that. The time had come for a total breakdown! Narelle went into her room, pulled the blinds down, threw herself on the bed and waited for the breakdown, sobbing uncontrollably. As she lay there, her three-year-old Krystle climbed up on the bed, plopped herself and an ice-cold kilo jar of yoghurt on her mother's stomach and pleaded with her mum to help her open it.

"Yoghurt", Narelle screamed, "I'm having a breakdown, and you talk to me about yoghurt!" Maybe aware that if she flung it, she'd still have to clean it up, Narelle ripped open the yoghurt and again awaited the breakdown. Suddenly she had a vision of Krystle falling over on her way back to the kitchen, so she jumped up, cursed the kids and the fact that she couldn't even have a breakdown in peace and decided that she would have to postpone her breakdown. With the help of neighbours and the local women's health centre, that breakdown is still on hold, but her love isn't. They're a family.

But sometimes, we need something special to remind us that we can cope. Narelle found that special something in this poem by the Argentinian poet, Jorge Luis Borges.

After a while you learn the subtle difference
Between holding a hand and chaining a soul,
And you learn that love doesn't mean leaning
And company doesn't mean security.
And you begin to learn that kisses aren't contracts
And presents aren't promises,
And you begin to accept your defeats
With your head up and your eyes open
With the grace of a woman, not the grief of a child,
And you learn to build all your roads on today
Because tomorrow's ground is too uncertain for plans
And futures have a way of falling down in mid-flight.
After a while you learn...
That even sunshine burns if you get too much.
So you plant your garden and decorate your own soul,
Instead of waiting for someone to bring you flowers.
And you learn that you really can endure...
That you really are strong
And you really do have worth...
And you learn and learn...
With every good-bye you learn.

I love that poem, and it's tragically true, isn't it? Only pain lets us understand pleasure, only rejection makes us savour acceptance, and only time can give us the wisdom to make sense of it all. Thank you Narelle. Sharyn and I welcome you to my Humble Heroes' Hall of Fame.

Editorial comment:
"All things will pass." So sang George Harrison, the Beatle perhaps most affected by Eastern religion and philosophy.
Many of us will experience sadness, pain, and anguish over a breakup or a rejection. If we are able to face these situations knowing that "all things will pass" then we are more likely to handle and overcome them.

"Awareness of impermanence and appreciation of our human potential will give us a sense of urgency that we must use every precious moment."
– Dalai Lama

Story 29

Paul

Paul was trying to give
me an urgent message but I didn't hear it

This story doesn't contain a good lesson, but it is an important lesson. Paul was one of my mature-age students. He used to follow me around, make sure he was in all my tutorial classes and come to my office often to have a chat about his assignments. To be honest, I got to the point where I did my best to avoid him. Had I been his counsellor rather than his lecturer, I might have handled the situation differently. Fortunately, Paul got a First Class Honours degree and then went overseas for his post-graduate studies. However, a couple of years later, I received this email from him.

> Dear Dr Irvine.
> Towards the end of my final year, I knew that you were trying to avoid me. I understand that, but because I looked up to you so much, I was hoping you could read my need and help me through my turmoil. After finishing my studies, I summoned the courage to see a counselor.
>
> Years later, I'm now sharing this letter with you in the hope it may help others and that something good may come out of my destructive experience. I was a victim of child abuse for several years. At the end of my Honours year, I summoned the courage to phone the man who had sexually abused me and asked him why. I wanted answers. I trembled as I asked, but his response really rattled me: "I regret it," he said.
>
> Thank God, I thought, for, in that statement, he admitted what he had done and was not proud of it. He called it an "affair". I wanted to vomit. An affair! With a ten-year-old child. The word affair implied complicity. There was no complicity. I never went along with it. It was pure abuse. He asked me to keep it to myself. NO! Not any more. I had kept quiet all my life, and the abuse had haunted me. No more. End of story.
> End of abuse. End of being a victim.
>
> Suddenly my life had changed forever. I was in control, and I felt powerful. I was free. After phoning my counsellor and sharing the breakthrough, I wrote the following:
>
> A Victim No More.
> The journey has ended, and I have left the train. It will travel on, and I don't know where.

Passengers are still on board, and new ones will be picked up.
A few will get off.
I am alone, standing at the station. I breathe the air and smell
the atmosphere.
Scared but powerful, the victim no more!
I don't need the train to pain as I have my own two feet. I am standing,
not sitting. Walking, not being carried.
Control, I am in control. The train had no driver or conductor and was out
of control.
The victim express will travel without me. A victim no more.

This episode had a massive influence on me. I let Paul down big time and hope I've been more sensitive since and more ready to down tools, drop the bureaucratic bustle and be prepared to hear that "inconvenient" truth. Paul deliberately left no return address, and I've not heard from him since. But Paul's journey has a message too about what it means to be a victim.

Editorial comment:
Becoming a victim is often something we have no control over, but being a victim is up to us. We do have a choice.

"No one saves us but ourselves. No one can and no one may. We ourselves must walk the path."
– Buddha

Story 30

Kim

Kim Beazley shares his personal story
about the power of his mother's attention

Celebrity Contribution

It may be hard for you to think of any politician as "humble", but this story emphasises the mother of none other than Kim Beazley, a name many readers will remember.

When Kim was the Federal Opposition leader and before he became Australia's Ambassador to the USA, I interviewed him for my "Who'd Be a Parent" book in his Sydney office. Regardless of party politics, Kim was an imposing man and one of the most impressive of the many famous faces I have caught up with in my many years in the media. We both loved cricket, so we got on famously.

My question to Kim at that time was, "What was the secret behind his success?" He just threw his ample body back in his ample chair and roared out laughing. His roar was because he said he felt a failure on so many fronts so often. Rarely, he said, would he go to bed satisfied that he had fulfilled his responsibilities.

If he had done the right thing as a parent, chances are he would have neglected his party, politics or policy. When I asked the question again, and he sensed I was serious, he looked reflectively up to the skies and said, "The top three factors in my life have been my mother's attention, second would be my mother's attention, and the third would be my mother's attention! My mother was a powerful influence in my background. She was a supportive influence. If ever there was something I wanted to do, she was right in there behind it. And so she was a strong mother, a good one, a very busy one, and I was damn lucky."

That got me reflecting on what motivated me and helped me handle complex cases, and I would have to say the same thing. It was mum's attention, and my brothers all felt the same. She wasn't a good cook or cleaner, we had no car, no money, and she never went to see me play sport, but we all knew where we were in her heart.

Alvin Toffler once said that, "Parenting remains the greatest single preserve of the amateur." We may have difficult kids, difficult partners, and difficult circumstances. We all feel a total failure at times, with no answers to the overwhelming challenges facing us every day, but if the kids are confident where they sit in our hearts, the rest can be repaired and recovered and rekindled with that great elixir, time.

So, swallow deep, hug hard and get back in the saddle! In today's busy world, that is not always possible, and I could tell you just as many stories about dads' hard yards and unconditional love, often against incredible odds, that have inspired me so much.

I'm writing this story for Mothers' Day, and my Humble Heroes are all those Mums who've given so much, for so many years, often in very lonely circumstances with heartache as their only companion and so often for so little thanks. So many of us are the beneficiaries of that selfless love. On behalf of Kim, myself, and probably every reader who has made it through life's labyrinth, thank you.

Editorial comment:
What a heartfelt story! We all need to be able to embrace failure and when we do make a mistake, take a moment to recognise what it is we did wrong, how to fix it, and how to avoid repeating our mistake in the future. If we gain something out of our mistake, it's not failure; it's a learning experience.
"Experience is simply the name we give our mistakes."
– Oscar Wilde

Series 4

31. Brenda – Brenda, my secretary, catches me out in a way that embarrasses me to this day

32. Damyon – Damyon had nothing going for him, time in jail and on the run – but the love of his step-sons makes him lift his game

33. Jane – a frustratingly funny (in the re-telling) story about Dr Jane trying to help out during Covid and being blocked by bureaucracy

34. Gordon – the Otto man learns a lesson in showing respect to his elders when he faces Australia's Over 70s cricket captain, Gordon

35. Jack – WorryWoo Squeek helps Jack settle into his new family life

36. Helen – despite severe medical setbacks, Helen goes on to head up a family that does her proud

37. Maria – Maria's daughter was sad and depressed but Maria thought it was all because she had lost her nana

38. Mr Wheeler – Mr Wheeler mightn't have been the best French teacher in the world but his commitment to his students had them performing as if he was

39. Noel – Noel gives us a different look at sustainability in his one teacher school – but what was he sustaining?

40. Celebrity contribution: John Howard – regardless of personal politics, no-one ever doubted John Howard's commitment to his family

Story 31

Brenda

My secretary catches me out in a
way that embarrasses me to this day

Circumstances unwittingly trap us into half-truths that exact their pound of moral flesh over the years. It may be skeletons in the closet, Santa faux pas, romantic clangers, or everyday things where you get sprung. It may even make you squirm to this day as you revisit the incredible chain of circumstances that snared you.

I still squirm over this one, and that's why it's in my memoirs. Brenda was my Irish secretary and a wonderful one at that – very thoughtful, organised, respectful, and never seemed to have a bad hair day. But Brenda had one glaring fault. She trusted me and thought I knew my stuff.

My crown came crashing down one Friday morning when Brenda decided to engage me in a friendly, easy social topic that could not offend anyone. (Note the ticks I've given myself for honesty along the way.)

The conversation went something like this.

> Brenda: "Good morning – what are you doing this weekend?" (√)
> Me: "Oh, taking Heather to Little Athletics tonight and having friends over tomorrow night." (√)
> Brenda: "Oh, that's nice. I suppose, like most Australian men I know, you'll be doing the barbecuing?" (√)
> Me: "I think so, but actually, I'm making a Pavlova for dessert." (√).
> Brenda: "Oh, that's interesting. I've heard people mention Pavlova, but I've never made one." (√)
> Me: "Yes, I gather they named the Pavlova, after a famous Russian ballerina, Anna Pavlova, who toured Australia and New Zealand in 1926. Both countries claim ownership of the term." (√)
> Brenda: "So how do you make it?" (A logical question, but now I'd set myself up as a know-all, I couldn't back down – the truth noose was tightening.)
> Me: "With eggs, and I beat them up into a fluffy ring and then after it's cooked, I put cream and fruit on top." (An OK answer, but I should have said "I gather" or words to that effect to indicate I had never made one before.)
> Brenda: "That's interesting, sounds yum. I gather you separate the egg

whites from the yolks. So what do you do with the yolks?" (Again, a legitimate question, but because I knew the background to the Pavlova and the ingredients, she assumed I was a Pavlova expert. I was going to make the Pavlova that weekend, and I had never made one before! But being her esteemed boss, I didn't think this was the time to disillusion her and figured I could bluff my way through and that Brenda would drop the subject – big mistake!)

Me:"Oh, I use the yolks, too. " (x)

Brenda:"How?" (√)

Me:"Oh, I put them on afterwards. " (x)

Brenda:"What do you mean? You put them on afterwards? Do you just drizzle them on or cook them, and where do you put them?" (√)

At this point, I broke down and confessed that I had never made one, that this was my first go, and I didn't have a clue or care what people did with the bloody yolks!! Then I stormed out of the office and never totally regained my crown again!

So, that's what can happen, my friends, when you let a half lie ruin your career. As the saying goes, "What a dangerous web we weave when we try a lady to deceive!" Lesson learnt. But I still shrivel at the memory!

> *Editorial comment:*
> *In this most entertaining story, Dr John mangles Walter Scott's "Oh, what a tangled web we weave" quote but gets the message across. Walter Scott refers to the memory-shrivelling effects of lying and how one lie leads to others. As the lies multiply, we become trapped in the sticky web of deceit.*
>
> *Often wrongly attributed to Shakespeare, the original excerpt from the poem Marmion is:"Oh, what a tangled web we weave when at first we start to deceive."*

Story 32

Damyon

Damyon had nothing going for him, time
in jail and on the run – but the love of his
step-sons makes him lift his game

This story begins with a whinge but ends up in triumph! Because there's no parenting licence and authorities appear petrified of being accused of usurping their role, people can inflict grossly incompetent and cruel parenting on children. It's the kids that suffer. We stand by and do nothing. They say it takes a village to raise a child, but too often, the villagers just cower and curse.

But worse, even when the safety of children forces "Welfare" to take the children away, the children are returned at the whim of an unstable parent, and the destructive cycle continues. With each relocation, the bonds get harder to forge, and the child's behaviour usually becomes more difficult to manage.

If we spent a fraction of the money in the early prevention/intervention years to help young, lost, lonely and troubled parents that we spend on housing our failures in more and more jails, we would make a difference. But, you cry, we don't have the resources. That's not true.

Damyon's story gives us hope and direction. Damyon is closer to 40 now. He has done time for a vicious assault on his wife's ex-boyfriend, and he's the sort of person to whom you'd never entrust children. How would you have fared had you had a childhood like Damyon's?

Damyon can't remember much about his childhood. Mum was an alcoholic, and dad used to beat her (and the kids) mercilessly. She died when Damyon was still at primary school. Damyon couldn't cope with dad (and apparently, nor could Welfare), so he took to the streets and fended for himself till the court had him locked up. That proved to be anything but a safe haven as the ex-boyfriend had a contract out with another inmate to dispose of Damyon.

But Damyon had one or two things going for him; he was a bright boy and a terrific footballer. He knew that what he had been doing was a stupid way to waste his life, even though he knew no other way.

Damyon met up with Narelle, who had two boys he adored, but even that couldn't stop his wayward life. They locked him up again. However, while in jail, he took to reading some self-help books, did some work experience in green-keeping and grounds management and was determined to find a better way to live.

What bugged Damyon most was that he had let down the two boys who worshipped the ground he walked on, particularly as their mother was locked away in a drug rehab program.

When Damyon got parole, he knew what he had to do. He had to win back these boys and prove to the court that he could. His football coach took him under his wing and got him some work at the oval, and Damyon took every course he could to learn how to love and be a good parent. Welfare finally let him take the boys back on a trial basis. The boys settled down incredibly well and very quickly. Damyon had little finesse in his fathering skills, but he had the basics – commitment, courage and the boys' respect. So far, so good and mum is now allowed out every second weekend to catch up with Damyon and the kids.

I remember Damyon's case, not just because of his sheer courage and tenacity against all odds but because I've always respected battlers. If you feel the same way, and if you have battlers in your life doing hard yards as mum or dad or step-parent or grandparent or foster carer, make sure you let them know how proud you are of the job they're doing – it can make all the difference!

I salute you, Damyon as an incredibly Humble Hero!

Editorial comment:
Damyon is the little Aussie battler personified. Dr John shows us that whingers and 'losers' can end up as winners if they persevere. Far-fetched? Literature has some great stories of losers becoming winners. Who would have thought that a humble peace-loving Hobbit would end up saving the world?

"The Hobbit is hallowed for his terrible and grace-filled journey and hollowed out by it. His body seems too small for all that he endures but not so his heart. Fear, fatigue, cold, hunger, and thirst torment him, but he continues out of love."
– Anne Marie Gazzolo, "Moments of Grace and Spiritual Warfare in The Lord of the Rings"

Story 33

Jane

A frustratingly funny (in the re-telling) story
about Dr Jane trying to help out during Covid
and being blocked by bureaucracy

We've all been stuck with the odd encounter or three with Bureaucracy! "Your call is important." "Would you prefer to chat online?" "Press 4 for us to call you back."

With all that in mind, you have to feel for Dr Jane. Jane is one of those very giving souls who doesn't count the cost. During Covid, she decided that, as a GP, she would contribute to the response to the crisis. She volunteered to administer the vaccine and expedite the rollout. Her frustration with the bureaucracy was so acute that it spilt out in a letter.

Dear John.

Having been out of General Practice for a few years, I complete the mandatory three-hour online training program for vaccinators (even though I've been giving vaccines for 40 years). To cut a long story short, I thought I should put my shoulder to the vaccine rollout and offer to help, as every centre was overwhelmed.

Our Practice Manager is told that I need to complete paperwork to enable me to work at the practice. "I'm happy to be voluntary", I suggest, but the response is "No", for legal reasons.

After much searching, we find my old Provider Number, so now I'm all set. Meanwhile, time is fast running out to help other doctors in the short-staffed weekend clinic.

"No," says bureaucracy, "That provider number is inactive. You must register with PRODA".

I start registering with PRODA. My home street as a child, favourite dog's name, school attended, Drivers' Licence, Medicare number, passport details – done. The clinic is on the following week. Thank God for that. "No," PRODA says, "The details don't match". Surprisingly my Medical Registration in my professional name is not required. I've always practised under my maiden name. My Drivers' Licence, however, is in my married name.

So begin the endless calls. The recorded voice tells me to be courteous in what I say, and they will be too. Now I need to submit my marriage certificate. Now, where would that be?

I speak to about six people, repeating my story each time. Each time I phone and try to talk to someone, after hanging on for ages again, we revisit the same details – the street I lived in, our dog's first name, and the school attended. Each time I am reminded to be courteous, and they will be too.

They realise, "You are not using your married name!" "No, I never have; I have always practised under my maiden name.""Ah, sorry, you must fill out a change of name form." My search doesn't bring up the correct form.

Finally, they tell me which form it is. I scan it and submit it with the marriage certificate. "Sorry, your Provider Number is not working. Please hold while we transfer you to the provider number department." I hold for another ten minutes. Then a "Senior Provider Number Consultant" informs me that my details aren't matching. I explain again, yet at no time do they ever ask me for my Medical Registration details.

It's two days before the clinic. Finally, after getting my local Federal Politician involved, I get through to a Senior Officer in the Department of Health. She needs my banking details. Right, I am done. PRODA now tells me to submit!! Ha, at last, finished!

"System unavailable," it tells me. I try three more times. Friday morning. Clinic tomorrow. I still can't submit my banking details. I ring PRODA again. They can't help. "Try Medicare to help with banking details."

Friday afternoon. At 4. 40 pm, a helpful Medicare lady changes old banking details to new ones. No form is needed! I send her flowers down the phone and a box of chocolates and champagne! Hallelujah. Their consultant phones me to ask if it has all gone smoothly! I splutter something back at him. Meanwhile, the office is due to close in 10 minutes, and it's still not fully resolved as I can't be "linked" to the GP Practice. Finally, I think that it's all sorted.

After two more calls and my blood pressure needing more medication, this gentleman suggests the problem may be that I'm using the wrong "link" number. It's the first time I've heard the word.

At that point, I have a total meltdown, and it's after five. I try to ring the surgery, but I get the answer machine. I phone the courteous consultant back and inform him "in no uncertain terms" that tomorrow I will be giving the jabs even if it is illegal, and I end up in jail! And I slam the phone down.

Saturday, I do the clinic. It's enjoyable. Patients are grateful.

Monday, PRODA calls back to check how things went!!

Dr Jane, could I just say it would be my absolute pleasure to visit you in jail and give you my Humble Heroes' Award for Perseverance! And I'd love to leave you with some platitude such as, if at first you don't succeed with bureaucracy, try a little "ardour". It's not easy to love something that has no heart. Maybe we just need to turn more to each other for those intangibles.

Editorial comment:
People often refer to Dr Jane's experience as being Kafkaesque, given that the Czech author is famous for his portrayals of the madness of bureaucracy. More accessible for many of us than Kafka, Douglas Adams and Terry Pratchett have also taken a swipe at red tape. In Pratchett's "Discworld", hell itself is one endless system of bureaucratic red tape, where they make doomed souls sit through every last codicil and sub-paragraph of the rules pertaining to Health and Safety – all 40,000 volumes of them.

Story 34

Gordon

The Otto man learns a lesson in showing respect
to his elders when he faces Australia's Over 70s
cricket captain, Gordon

Do you have anyone in your life who's a bit old, wrinkly, stiff, and nowhere near what they used to be? I suppose the older I get, the more aware I've become of how easy it is to be written off as aged and irrelevant. And I think it's a fact that with the speed of infotech expansion, the older generation has even less to offer in the way of accumulated knowledge and wisdom from the past. Many of us are so stupid we can't even navigate through computer problems, the Internet, the Password changes, the impersonal Virtual help we're offered, or the humiliating hold online when they say, "Contact us because your call is important".

The world has changed, and the tribe has changed. In our younger days, we looked up to our seniors because they knew so much. Now, knowledge is all on their devices – no need to look up to us. Just look down at their devices.

I'm sure you could match my frustration many times over. But now let me introduce the Otto man and Gordon, the cricket tragic. I admit to being a bit of a cricket enthusiast myself, but these days I watch more than I play. On this occasion, our Seniors' cricket team was practising in the nets at Fagan's Park, and I was sitting on the benches outside the oval, just about to change into my cricket gear. Along came the Otto man. He dismounted from his truck cabin, came to the bin beside me, said "Hi", and noticed all our team practising in the nets. "Heh, that's a good idea getting the oldies out like that. What retirement village would they all be from, mate?"

"Actually, they're all living independently, and they're very talented cricketers," I replied, maybe a bit abruptly. "See that white-haired guy who's putting his pads on over there? That's Gordon, and he's been the Australian Over-70s cricket captain. And that guy who just bowled that ball? Well, he happens to be the opening bowler in Gordon's team. " Then I buried my head, trying to put my cricket boots on and hiding my hurt. The Otto man stopped in his tracks, looked back at the motley mob and simply said, "Well, I'll be buggered. "

He just saw older men filling in their day. He didn't see Gordon, the young fella who represented the Coast in his younger days. He didn't see the esteem the rest of us had for him. He didn't know that Gordon had had two knee operations and was riddled with arthritis. Gordon could still bat well but struggled to run between the two wickets. However, he could still get us all there for net practice, select and organise teams to play around the state, and come alongside others there who were struggling with fitness or family. The Otto man just saw old men.

Gordon doesn't know he's my humble hero. Maybe I should tell him. And perhaps you could tell a few of the lost, lonely ones you know and maybe listen to their stories of times past, before time passed by them. Keep in mind that our kids will treat us the way they saw us treat our oldies.

In the fast, furious world we're living in, never has there been more need to nurture and nourish. And maybe those in the older bracket could spend less time dreaming of past glories and remember that a listening ear, a word of encouragement and an arm over the shoulder can never be outdated. So let's play a captain's knock, like Gordon, even from the sidelines. We don't need to run, just stand still and support.

Editorial comment:
Good on you Dr John. Here's a quick blast on a similar theme from my favourite band.

"Don't have to be ashamed of the car I drive (at the end of the line)
I'm just glad to be here, happy to be alive (at the end of the line)
And it don't matter if you're by my side (at the end of the line)
I'm satisfied
Well, it's alright, even if you're old and grey
Well, it's alright, you still got something to say
Well, it's alright, remember to live and let live
Well, it's alright, the best you can do is forgive."
– The Travelling Wilburys

Story 35

Jack

WorryWoo Squeek helps Jack
settle into his new family life

$\mathcal{I}$ could hear the panic in mum's voice. "What's going on with my lovely boy? He's such a good kid, does well at school, got plenty of friends, but this year, it has been a nightmare. Jack went off OK on the first day of the year, and I thought we were off to a good start, but it has worsened. Now I can't get him to school. He won't sleep in his bed and screams if I try to force him to go to school. Every night he promises me he will be good the next day, but it's always the same. He says he's sick, but the doctors say it's just "school sick" – for some reason, he's allergic to school this year!"

I had known of young Jack for a year when mum came to see me after separating from Jack's dad. Rochelle had packed up and come to live near her mother and family. But Jack had handled the transition well and had managed the new school. OK, so what had gone wrong?

Like everything in life, the problem was a bit complicated – new teacher, new classmates, fighting between mum and his much-loved dad, but the catalyst was a kid in his class called Liam who was giving Jack a hard time at school. Jack couldn't cope, and the situation crushed his confidence.

I managed to get dad onside and aware of his son's stress. There had to be many sides to his recovery. We got Jack's teacher to give him a particular job in the morning, and she changed his seating so he was near his mate. Then she got Liam and Jack together for a "negotiation" session. It turned out that Liam thought Jack didn't like him, so at least they've made their peace for the moment.

But I had great success with Squeek. I happened to have all the WorryWoos in my room at the clinic, and Jack took a fancy to Squeek. That suited me because Squeek was the creature who was scared of trying anything new, so he hid out at home. We read the Andi Green book, "The Monster in the Bubble", and then I offered Jack an incentive. I told him he could take Squeek home and keep him as long as he showed me he was doing brave things to make Squeek proud.

Jack seemed keen to have a go, so we made a list of things he could do to show me he deserved to keep Squeek. That included achievements like staying in his bed (or Squeek would be lonely), going to school with Nana (as he got too upset leaving mum), trying new foods, going to his cousins' place and staying for a while without mum.

Jack's doing well, and he still has Squeek!

Jack, you'll do me as a young Humble Hero. You took on forces too strong for you and found a way to out-trump them.

Editorial comment:
Worry and fear are different forms of anxiety. Fear usually happens in the present. Worry usually happens when a child thinks about past or future situations.

"I thought that if I owned nothing, had nothing, was nothing, I would have nothing left to lose, and I wouldn't be scared anymore. Because my whole life, I've been so damn scared. Scared to live because I was scared to die. But at the same time I was so scared of living, so I wanted to die."
– Charlotte Eriksson, "Empty Roads & Broken Bottles: In Search For The Great Perhaps"

Story 36

Helen

Despite severe medical setbacks,
Helen goes on to head up a family that
does her proud

As you can perhaps tell by the name, Helen grew up in the last century. But regardless of how old you are, everyone would love someone like Helen in their family. Helen was born into a well-to-do family. Everything was going fine for Helen – her schooling, and her beloved horse, Judy, which she rode to school. She planned to become a pioneering female teacher like her mother and grandmother, and then she was struck down with Scarlet Fever. And at 16, Helen was told she would never walk again. But the impossible was just another challenge for Helen.

After a year in isolation in a dark room at home, Helen got back up, finished her teacher training and became a teacher. Then as women had to do in those days, Helen gave up her career to have children after marrying a righteous God-fearing man named Alex. No Sunday sport or cooking or even reading the paper; Sunday was God's day.

Helen's Scarlet Fever had left her with a weak heart, so housework and spouse work were hard, especially as they had no car.

Helen didn't even have enough money to buy shoes for the boys' feet, but with pure determination, she got back into teaching and became the first female casual teacher appointed after the war.

Helen lost her much-adored dad to a diabetic stroke early in her married life. Then, just as the family was getting back on their feet, Helen's mother developed senility. In those days, the care of the elderly, regardless of their mental or physical health, fell to the children. Helen's sister would have nothing to do with this role, so Helen took her mum in and saw her through her increasingly difficult final years until she passed away.

All four boys followed in their mother's footsteps and became teachers. They then took up appointments scattered across NSW and in PNG. There was no email in those dim, dark days, and phone calls were costly, so Helen would write a letter to the boys, with one boy getting the original and the other three getting carbon paper copies. The daughters-in-law shared the adoration her boys felt towards their mum, so despite the poor financial start and a dogmatic dad, the family stayed united.

As for the boys, knowing they had the unconditional love and support of their mum, each used that solid foundation as a springboard into incredible roles of service in the community. The eldest stayed teaching but became head of the Gideon Bible distribution program. The next became an academic, serving many years with UNICEF and successfully promoting education for girls throughout Asia. The youngest brother became a neuropsychologist. We set up the READ clinic together, and I have become a Paediatric Psychologist!

Helen, we welcome you to a place of honour in our Humble Heroes' Hall of Fame. That family was no more special or talented than any other family. Still, all four boys, their partners, their children, and their children's children have all been touched by this lady and her attitude of gratitude. Individual family members may pass away, but what they weave into the souls of those they meet and leave behind is a strong fabric that lasts well beyond their lifetime.

If you have an unsung hero in your life, don't let them remain unsung. It's no accident that you have inherited many of their attributes. Contact them, write to them or tell your family all about them.

Editorial comment:
Such a simple but such a powerful story. Very brave, too, of Dr John to offer the reader such an intimate glimpse into his inner family. I love his reflections on love and loss and how people "weave into the souls of those they meet".

Emily Dickinson is regarded by some as the poet laureate of love and loss. Writing in nineteenth-century America in the aftermath of the Civil War, Dickinson's poetry shows grief as an experience both profoundly intimate and profoundly universal.
"I measure every Grief I meet
With narrow, probing, Eyes –
I wonder if It weighs like Mine –
Or has an Easier size."

Story 37

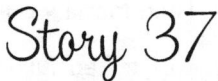

Maria

Maria's daughter was sad and depressed
but Maria thought it was all because she
had lost her Nana

Kids come in strange little bundles, and I'd never know what surprises each little bundle had in store for me when they came in through that clinic door. Six-year-old Jessica looked fit and well, but a sense of sadness in her eyes was evident immediately.

Her mum, Maria, said Jessica had been crying a lot, wouldn't play with other kids and had become very clingy. Maria was sure that she was depressed about the loss of her Grandma, who had died suddenly three years before. Every time Jessica was sad and crying, and Maria asked her what was wrong, she'd say she missed her Nana. Then Maria would burst into tears.

The oddest thing emerged when I talked further and did some doll play with Jessica alone. Jessica hardly knew her Grandma! What also occurred was that Maria hadn't been in touch with her mum for over a month before her sudden death. Previously Maria and her mum had been very close, but there had been a falling out over the behaviour of Maria's partner.

What was really going on was that Jessica was grieving, not over nana, but over missing the lost happiness in her home. In a way, since nana's death, she had emotionally really lost her mum.

The sudden loss of loved ones leaves so much unfinished business that we're caught in for an eternity. There's no time to say "I'm sorry", "I love you", or "Don't go yet", or "Let me tell you what you've meant to me".

Although it's small comfort, nobody, no matter how close or prepared they may have been for the loss, ever really escapes this feeling. It's part of the "if only. . . " stage that follows soon after the denial and the anger stages. It takes the mind but a moment to turn from blame to shame; in fact, this very stage of unbearable anguish marks the beginning of our adjustment to the loss.

In her (out of print) Millenium Press book "No Time For Goodbyes", Janice Harris Lord suggests that if you've lost a mate suddenly and haven't had time to say everything you wanted, then take time to communicate even now. For some, that might be prayer; for others, it might be writing a letter to the one you've lost and even writing a reply. It's not weird. Grieving is doing whatever you need to help you understand and accept. As the anguish decreases, then so will the letters.

As we age, the pain and anguish of lost loves can give us serenity and understanding way beyond the tumult and the shouting of a world in torment. It's called maturity.

Maria had not done her grieving. She was so determined to deny the pain that she had passed it on to her daughter. It's worth remembering that grieving is the only form of pain that comforts.

If this strikes a chord in your life, and you have unfinished grieving, then do it in any form that feels right. Just don't bury it. Be proud of your memories and treasure what that person has meant to you – that's what they would want more than anything else.

Editorial comment:
Sometimes in times of grief, the words of other, more articulate people can soothe the pain. Can their eloquence help us to comprehend suffering? There is no scientific evidence that either confirms or denies the proposition, but I'm with Dr John on this one – don't bury your grieving.

"No, don't stop writing your grievous poetry.
It will do you good, this work of your grief.
Keep writing till there is nothing left.
It will take time, and the years will go by."
– Douglas Dunn, on his wife's death, from "December in Elegies" (1995)

Story 38

Mr Wheeler

Mr Wheeler mightn't have been the best French teacher in the world but his commitment to his students had them performing as if he was

*J*ust recently I've been back to Bathurst to celebrate our 60-year reunion. It was 62 years, but Covid postponed the event as it did to so many worthwhile and important celebrations. As I mixed with old colleagues, I couldn't get over how many aged teachers, in the twilight years of their life, could confidently and comfortably reel off the names of fellow teachers and pupils who had significantly impacted their lives. So just for today, think back to the most memorable teachers you had through school, and what was it about them that made them so special?

Was it that they were just brilliant exponents of their subject area? Or was it the fact that they cared? My French teacher, Mr Wheeler, profoundly affected me – not because he was brilliant but because he cared. He not only liked kids, but he also took our tennis team on Sports Days and went with us all over Sydney to play.

I wanted to thank Mr Wheeler because I worked hard in that subject and did better in French than in any other subject. I still keep in touch with a great group of boys (old men) who went to Fort Street with me, and every one of them speaks in hushed tones about their Maths teacher, Mr Coroneos. Indeed, such was the influence Jimmy Coroneos had on their lives that many of them went into Maths-related careers such as Engineering, Accountancy and Architecture or became Maths teachers themselves.

It's a fact that, as parents get busier and the world gets more complex, we seem to want teachers to fix it all – behaviour, IT, multi-culturalism, sex education, bullying, gender equity, gender fluidity – and we pay them relatively little for the privilege. A teacher from Western Australia, Rod Clarke, puts it this way:

When society has a problem, a matter of import,
It must be taught in schools, they say, or something of the sort.
Traffic mayhem on our roads, there are too many fools –
Bicycle safety, that's the trick – it must be taught in schools!
Too many drownings at our beaches, right across the nation,
Let's teach the kids in all the schools about resuscitation.
I see the future clearly now, as if through crystal glass.
A vast array of problems solved, as through the schools they pass.
Table manners, sexual conduct, coping with divorce.

Anti-smoking, prejudice, and conservation of course.
Children hooked on television? Parents don't you frown,
The school can teach them how to cut their viewing hours down.

I know there'll be complaints about this passing of the buck,
But just ignore those teachers now, it's really their bad luck,
They always whinge and moan, you know, they really are so trite,
They even want to teach the kids to count and read and write!
Now reading's fine and grammar, too, and all those spelling rules,
But really now, I ask you this, must they be taught in schools?

What a privilege it has been to be a teacher. People may better remember me as a Paediatric Psychologist, but the confidence teaching gave me allowed me to connect with many families over many years. Thanks kids, and although you've passed on, thanks Mr Wheeler.

Maybe if you've had a teacher who profoundly impacted you, Google them and let them know. Judging by the reaction of my Bathurst colleagues, those few words could do more to lift their ailing spirits than any medication could ever achieve.

Editorial comment:
The media informs me that morale within the teaching profession is at an all-time low. Children in the post-Covid school environment are demoralised and disconnected; having a teacher feeling the same way reinforces it. When people are feeling discouraged, it can be contagious. Let's do what Dr John suggests and thank a teacher.

"Piglet noticed that even though he had a Very Small Heart, it could hold a rather large amount of Gratitude."
– A.A. Milne

Story 39

Noel

Noel gives us a different look at
sustainability in his one teacher school –
but what was he sustaining?

You know the buzzword now in Education is Sustainability, and rightly so, or the kids won't have a decent planet on which to live. Maybe schools near you have picked up the mantle and come up with good projects. The local school is gearing up to water tanks and solar energy, and having every class develop their vegetable patch and recycling is all the go, as it should be.

These are great ideas but very different to my school experience with sustainability! When I was training to be a teacher in small country schools, one near Bathurst took the prize for economic ingenuity – happy kids, delighted parents and one relatively rich teacher. The Practice Teaching Coordinator sent me to this school, little realising, surely, what I'd be learning from this maestro of sustainable education!

I first noticed that Noel, the teacher, had about 20 sheep in his large playground, each stamped large with O S (On Service).

The second thing I observed was that Noel immediately dispatched several children to gardening duties after singing the anthem to start the day. These children were not good at schoolwork! Then Noel posted two academic strugglers to check on the sheep and assigned another child to the verandah. This boy was the "cockatoo" who had to report any sightings of the Inspector or the Practice Teaching Supervisor. He didn't rotate the roles, but members of the gardening squad were allowed back into the classroom after lunch for more practical subjects – so most kids got a turn doing something for the collective good.

At least twice a year, Noel would take the produce to the markets in Bathurst and dispatch the sheep to the stockyards. He would have a big weekend living it up in Bathurst on half the proceeds. The other half went to the P and C! So, no one thought of him as greedy or selfish. No, Noel had the welfare of the school at heart!

The parents were thrilled that their children were getting a "well-rounded" practical education. Not only that, but Noel had also been a panel beater before he went into teaching. Noel could fix any dings or scrapes or even do car servicing and save the locals a trip into town! The fact that his teaching methods were a little unorthodox and could hardly be called remedial didn't worry them. Indeed the thought of someone reporting Noel for lack of attention to curriculum guidelines was anathema because the kids were happy. If any parent dobbed him in, the net effect was that they would well lose their P and C income and their panel beater!

Concepts of sustainability have changed radically and for the better. Back then, it was Noel's lifestyle that he was sustaining! However, Noel argued that it was the small rural community that he was sustaining. Whatever your circumstances or philosophy, I hope your school is actively campaigning for sustainable futures and doing practical projects to make it happen. If not, maybe offer the school a hand to get things underway. We all can and need to do better to allow our kids to enjoy this wonderful world in which we live.

Noel, I couldn't say you were my Humble Hero, but I know you were a legend to many struggling farmers.

If you have someone at your school doing great things for the environment, then let me hear their story, and they can rightfully claim a place in the Humble Heroes' Sustainable Hall of Fame.

Editorial comment:
A few years ago, I was lucky enough to spend a few days at the Green School in Bali, where a friend of mine, John Stewart, was the Principal. Green School's mission of "a community of learners making our world sustainable" sets the core philosophy of why and how the School educates: to prepare learners for the real world by equipping them with knowledge, values and skills to navigate an ever-changing world.

Story 40

John

Regardless of personal politics, no one ever
doubted John Howard's commitment to his family

Celebrity Contribution

$\mathcal{P}$robably the favourite line of communication between workers, or at least Type A personalities, would be, "How are you? Busy?" That demonstrates one's success in climbing the bureaucratic ladder to whatever.

But if you think you're "busy," just how busy would you feel if you were the PM? As Kim Beazley bemoaned, the leader has to try to do the right thing by his parenting, party, politics, policies, colleagues and country. Surely the Prime Minister is entitled to call himself busy?

John Howard, our ex PM, was busy, but regardless of your politics, everyone on both sides of the chamber knew where they stood and where he stood. His commitment to his country, values and family were his unshakeable anchors. John agreed to contribute when I wrote my book "Who'd Be a Parent?". This extract reminds me why so many admired him.

My first question to him was, "Being so busy, how do you balance parenting and public life?"

> When Janette and I first discussed the realities of a political career and the possible effects on our family, we resolved that the most important consideration was to provide a stable and loving environment for our children.
>
> I often recall the advice given to me as a new Member of Parliament by Peter Nixon, a former Minister in the Fraser government. He spoke of the importance of the family. "Stay in touch every day and if you say you'll be home for something, be there."
>
> Politics is such an all-consuming thing for a family. Some of the hardest times for Janette and me as parents were to see our children disturbed by the publicity surrounding me during the difficult times, but as a family, we have always discussed the issues and got through them together. We have also shared the successes and challenges of my political career.

I then questioned John Howard on his techniques to survive the hard times.

> Very often, the hard times begin to look like the good times because they are the times that people who love each other pull together. Most parents find that their children get caught up in their challenges or problems. This is inevitable. Naturally, children worry about their parents – probably more than many parents realise. As parents, we all have to watch this and ensure that our children know we value their love, help and concern.

I then asked the PM for any tips as a busy parent.

I believe that bringing up children is the most important thing most people do in their lives, and nothing replaces time spent with your children. Encourage them in their endeavours, cheer their successes, and give them your shoulder when they don't succeed.

Good parents teach their children the values they will live by. These might be ordinary things like the value of work, earning a living, preparing for the future, managing what they have and sharing it when they can, and facing reality front on in the good times and the bad. For example, we have encouraged our children to have some degree of self-sufficiency that comes with earning their own pocket money through after-school jobs, and I know that they have learned through this.

There is probably only one thing more important than teaching your children, and that is learning from them. Many of the valuable lessons I have learned in the past 23 years have come simply from talking to my children and watching them grow. You must always take the time to talk, no matter how busy you are.

No need for me to say a thing. John Howard, thank you for your impressive role in my memoirs. Welcome to our Humble Heroes' Hall of Fame.

Editorial comment:
Your editor, dear reader, grew up in the 60s and it's the music of that era that often comes to mind. As I read this story, I was reminded of the Crosby, Stills and Nash classic, "Teach Your Children Well".
"And feed them on your dreams
The one they pick's the one you'll know by
Don't you ever ask them, "Why?"
If they told you, you would cry
So just look at them and sigh
And know they love you."

John Howard is right on the money, isn't he? The one thing more important than teaching your children is to learn from them.

Series 5

Story 41

Reg

Step-dad Reg steps up for Peter in an awesome
display of love and commitment

My story about Damyon featured a step-dad on the wrong side of the law who changed his whole life around because of his love for his step-sons.

Reg is a man cast or thrust into a similar role but so memorable I can still see his face, smirk and moustache, which was uncommon among plasterers. Reg will never get an AO, OAM or any medal because he's too busy looking after Peter – but what a job he's done.

Reg was a knock-about character but an excellent and tidy plasterer. I know that "good tidy plasterer" could be considered an oxymoron but not Reg.

He met Trixie, a single mum with a young son, Peter. They had both lived most of their life in country NSW.

I've never met Trixie. I tried to, but by the time I caught up with Reg, Trixie had found another man, and they had gone off to live in Tasmania – to set up a diet food delivery service.

Trixie passed Peter across to Reg as she left and said, "You love him so much, he's yours," leaving Reg with the boy and the bills.

When I caught up with Reg, Peter was about six. Reg's problem was that Trixie now wanted Peter back. (Have you heard this type of scenario before?) And Trixie was prepared to take Reg to court to get her way.

Reg was not going to let Peter go lightly. Peter hardly knew his mother and had had no contact with Trixie since she left, and from what I could gather, they didn't have a strong bond in the first place.

Although Reg had minimal legal clout because, after all, he was not blood-related, he had the backing of the school, and he had my support. I could see what a healthy, loving bond he and Peter had.

Reg was encouraged to stay strong by his new partner, who could also see they were like peas in a pod. We put in reports, and his barrister took it on.

It transpires that both before and after leaving Peter, Trixie had severe mental health issues. These resulted, in part, in volatile relationships.

After a two-year battle, which Reg could hardly afford, he won custody and brought Peter in, not just to thank me but to get some directions as to the best high school for his boy. My rooms were on the second floor of a four-storey building in Baker Street, Gosford.

After they both left to get dinner ready, I looked out the window and there they were, heading for the car park opposite. Peter was still happy to hold Reg's hand as they crossed the road, and then he jumped along the path avoiding the cracks.

I tell you, I had a huge lump in my throat, and my eyes would not stop watering up. What a great outcome, but I wonder what the cost was.

Reg is still a plasterer, but his much taller apprentice is none other than Peter, still with the same Cheshire cat grin and dreamy eyes. They're going well, but I wonder how many nights Reg would have turned in bed after Trixie left, wondering how to handle this convoluted mess.

I salute you, Reg, and I salute all those parents, step-parents, grandparents and foster carers who put themselves in harm's way for the sake of kids. Love does win through, sooner or later, one way or another.

Editorial comment:
We all know of situations where love was not strong enough to win through, but you have to love Dr John's enthusiastic optimism in this story. The apt quote is from an unlikely source; Godwin was an anarchist and the father of Mary Shelley, who wrote Dracula!

"Love conquers all difficulties, surmounts all obstacles, and effects what to any other power would be impossible."
– William Godwin

Story 42

Cassie

A lovely story about Cassie the
Collie proving that pets have feelings too

A neighbour read a story in a magazine and related it to me. The story's writer lived in a comfortable neighbourhood where everybody "minded their own business" and gossiped about everyone else's business.

Every afternoon, this well-groomed, well-fed dog turned up at the lady's front door, begging to come in. The lady obliged, and the dog flopped, exhausted and then disappeared again after dinner. This event became an everyday occurrence, and the dog would drop in, flop and then return as mysteriously as it had arrived.

After a few weeks of this drop-in and flop routine, the lady pinned a note to the dog saying, "I would like to know who the owner of this sweet dog is, and ask if you are aware that almost every afternoon your dog comes to my house for a nap".

The next day the dog arrived with a different note pinned to his collar. "He lives in a home with six children, two under the age of 3. He's trying to catch up on his sleep. Can I come with him tomorrow?"

This amusing story reminded me of a clinic case I had. This story is about a dog called Cassie and a girl named Amy.

Amy has to rank as one of the most active three-year-old kids I've ever seen, and I've seen a few. But she was not only active; Amy was downright dangerous.

She had no fear, no fear of heights, no fear of cars, no fear of knives, and no fear of dogs. But as this isn't a diagnostic or how-to-fix-it book, I won't go into the treatment we undertook, but their dog Cassie left its mark in my memories.

It turns out that mum and dad weren't the only ones struggling to cope with Amy; so was Cassie, their Border Collie.

Those of you who have a dog, especially a Border Collie, as we had as kids, will know just how tolerant they are!

Being a good-natured creature, Cassie couldn't yell, bite or even bark out her frustration with this dynamo who hugged, kicked, fell on her, and screamed in her ear.

So what did Cassie do? She buried everything that smelled of Amy. One day mum found Amy's Tele-Tubby buried in the garden with only the antennae showing,

But the story doesn't stop there. Cassie would even go to the dirty washing, sniff out anything that was Amy's and bury it, and the poor kid was forever running out of gear, or the garden fork discovered it.

The good news is that Amy did improve, and mum was impressed, but not Cassie! Mum reported that even recently, Cassie brought her lead to mum, dumped it at her feet, and then looked straight across at Amy.

Mum was sure she was trying to communicate that this kid needed that lead more than this Collie!

So, thank you to all the adorable pets that keep us sane. You are very Humble Heroes!

Editorial comment:
Writing in "The Guardian" during Covid, a journalist reported on pets' positive impact on people locked down in their homes.

"At no point in human history have so many pets been so important to so many people. We used to have stable jobs and a stable world. Now we just have stable pets – that are keeping many of us sane."
– Jules Howard

Story 43

Christine

Christine writes in with a timely reminder
that life is short and to slow down

$\mathcal{I}$'ve never met some of the people who make an impact on me. As many of you may remember, I had a syndicated spot on radio across the country for many years. We called it "Coping with Kids". I received an email from Christine after sharing the poem "Slow Dance" by David Weatherspoon on one such episode – so many years ago now.

Dear Dr John,

I gained a copy of the poem you shared through the station and felt it should be shared with your readers.

Have you ever watched kids On a merry-go-round
Or listened to the rain slapping on the ground?

Ever followed a butterfly's erratic flight
Or gazed at the sun into the fading light?
You better slow down. Don't dance so fast
Time is short. The music won't last.

Do you run through each day on the fly
When you ask, "How are you?"
do you hear the reply?

When the day is done, do you lie in your bed
With the next hundred chores
running through your head?

You'd better slow down. Don't dance so fast
Time is short. The music won't last.

Ever told your child, We'll do it tomorrow
And in your haste, not seen his sorrow?

Ever lost touch? Let a good friendship die
'Cause you never had time to call and say "Hi"?

You'd better slow down. Don't dance so fast
Time is short. The music won't last.

Life is not a race, do take it slower
Hear the music Before the song is over.

For me, the poem had particular poignance as it reminded me so much of a lesson I learnt after my mum died. As dad and I were painfully cleaning out her things, dad found a wrapped parcel with brand new never-been-worn lingerie with an astronomical price tag still on it.

"Your mum bought this in town at least eight or nine years ago. She never wore it." His hands lingered on the material for a moment, and he said, "Don't ever save anything for a special occasion. Every day you're alive is a special occasion." I'm still thinking about his words, which have changed my life. I'm reading more and dusting less. I'm sitting on the deck and admiring the view without fussing about the weeds in the garden. I spend more time with my family and friends and less in committee meetings. We use our good china and crystal for every special event, such as losing a kilo, getting the email to work again, and smelling the first camellia blossom.

"Someday" and "one of these days" are losing their grip on my vocabulary. If it's worth seeing, hearing, or doing, I want to see and hear and do it now. I'm not sure what my mum would've done had she known that she wouldn't be here for the tomorrow we all take for granted. I think she would have called family members and a few close friends. She might have called a few former friends to apologise and mend fences for past squabbles. I like to think she would have gone out for a Chinese dinner, her favourite food.

I'm guessing I'll never know.

Thanks for the memories, Christine. I hope we can all take stock of our lot through your thoughtful reminder. No matter what the hassles with parents or kids we're experiencing right now, strangely enough, in ten years, we'll look back and say these were the good years.

Story 44

Frank

An incredible but absolutely true story about how young Frank learns to convert his anger into art in a most unique way

How do you handle it when you get stirred up? What do you do? Is it destructive? Do you just go to tears? Do you go off into your cave and wait till you've calmed down? Or can you turn it into something constructive?

Last week I was up on my brother-in-law's farm, and he had this dead tree that had crashed to the ground a couple of years ago. It was huge, and Alan didn't have the energy to cut off the roots and cut up the trunk into small enough rings to move it. The superheroes in the movies seem to be able to do it – to use their anger to spur them into some heroic action.

But while I was up there, there was a minor "domestic incident", as we all have! Alan got very frustrated and angry with his wife, Leanne. He went off "into his quiet cave" for a bit. Then, he went out to that huge tree with a chainsaw and truck and chains. He removed the roots, pulled them back into the vertical with tow rope and truck and started cutting up the trunk rings. All of which had been beyond his energies for two years.

That little family incident brought back to mind one of the strangest and most incredible memories I have as I look back on a fortunate life. It's a remarkable and true story about eight-year-old Frank.

When he was in the local school, he had stabbed kids with his pencil, smashed chairs over other kids who had annoyed him, and upturned tables. He had bitten one teacher and kicked another so hard that she had to have time off teaching. Not surprisingly, Frank was offered alternate educational accommodation!

When I met Frank, he was quietly doodling away in a special school for disturbed kids. His remarkable, unflappable teacher, Craig, could see good in every child. As an aside, we were there to check the progress of Kurt. They had removed him from his public school for a similar style of acting out and swearing. Kurt's language would make a bullocky blush.

Craig was pleased with Kurt's progress, although his language was still foul. Craig was not perturbed at all. "No, we're making great progress. When Kurt was first admitted, he was swearing every second word; now it's every fourth!"

Silly me hadn't noticed.

Anyhow, back to the main story. As we went past Frank's desk, Craig stopped and asked Frank if he could draw a picture for "our visitor" (me!).

In front of me on my desk, to this very day, is the pencil drawing Frank did so many years ago. It's a fabulous sketch of a boy dragon pleading with an evil-looking mother dragon for the big grub she has in her mitt.

It's awesome because I watched Frank draw it. He did it in under one minute, starting from the mother's tail up around down, linking up exactly where he'd started as if he had traced it.

Craig said all Frank's drawings were the same – only drawn in anger, consistently fast and perfect and always vicious.

Frank loved trucks. Frank's dad, not surprisingly, was a truckie! However, dad's domestic violence towards his wife forced dad to leave home, and a restraining order meant no contact with the family.

Frank missed dad and his truck big time and took out his frustration in the only way he had seen and knew how – with violence!

However, the teachers in the special school had noticed his incredible artistic talent. They armed him with a huge pile of blank paper and sketching pencils.

They played up his love of animals to bring out his softer side and gradually got him to accept a cuddle which helped earth his "emotional electricity". They rewarded him for going to pencil and paper as soon as he was hurt, before he could hurt anyone else.

Three years later, when I next heard of Frank, he was back in the normal class, but he doesn't draw much these days. The truth is, Frank doesn't need to now because he only ever drew with such vivid imagery when he was angry.

The court has decreed that Frank can go out in dad's truck at weekends, which seems to have settled him down. And strangely enough, Frank doesn't mind being a non-drawer now. He likes it just the way it is! Maybe someday he'll return to it if some talented teacher can tap into his gift.

Well done, Frank, and thanks for the memories and my dragons!

Editorial comment:
Many artists use experiences from their own lives to create their art,
just like Frank. Some experts call this art form therapeutic or cathartic
as it allows the artist to use their pain to heal their wounds. Vincent
van Gogh was a famous exponent of the technique.

"Creating art can be a cathartic experience; an expression of many
intense emotions without ever saying a word. When emotions are
externalized through art, they are less debilitating and coping with
problems is a less overwhelming endeavour. "
— Sara Feinberg, (Art therapist)

Story 45

Jimmy

A salute to the great teachers and the impact those
teachers make on a child's life and career

Podcast Listener's Humble Hero

$\mathcal{I}$n one of my Humble Heroes podcasts, I asked listeners to drop me a line about a teacher who inspired them to the point that it affected their whole career. And what was it about them that made such an impact? Was it their charismatic personality, knowledge of their subject, discipline, looks, thorough preparation or the fact that they cared about you and went the extra mile?

But I've just had an email from Bruce, an old schoolmate at Fort Street, whom Jimmy Coroneos taught, and it reads this way.

> Dear Dr John,
>
> I've been listening to a few of your Humble Heroes stories and heard Jimmy Coroneos' name mentioned. I was one of the fortunate students who was taught by this remarkable man, and in no small way, he had a huge impact on my life.
>
> Jim was born in Gunning NSW, the son of Greek immigrant parents from the Island of Kythera. Jim was educated at the local Primary school, then Goulburn High, before gaining a scholarship to Sydney University.
>
> I first met Jim when he was my Mathematics teacher at Fort Street Boys High School in 1957.
>
> Passion, energy and focus were Jim's hallmarks, and he passed these values on to his students. We knew he cared whether we understood our mathematics basics. Jim's legacy was his effort in the lesson, his preparation beforehand and, of course, his deep interest in each of his Maths students.
>
> I remember Jim pacing back and forth across the raised platform at the front of our classroom as he explained a mathematical principle before turning to the blackboard to write down an equation in his copperplate hand. He produced endless sheets of mathematics problem sheets for us as homework. It was heads down to complete these sheets, but you knew if you did the work, you would be rewarded by good results.
>
> Jim Coroneos' homework sheets were so good they were later published as Mathematics textbooks for all NSW schools.
>
> With passion and energy, he also coached our Fort Street 2nd XV to the

final of the Rugby comp in 1958, which we lost to a Catholic team. I can still remember his voice from the sidelines in the final, urging us on to "pick up the bloody ball".

Most of Jim's Mathematics 1 and 2 A class at Fort Street achieved an Honours pass in the 1958 Leaving Certificate, setting some sort of a record.

This Honours ranking looked good on my CV and was a significant factor in gaining an Engineering Cadetship with CSR, with whom I stayed for almost 30 years.

One afternoon in 1959, in my first year of Engineering at Sydney University, my schoolmate Bill Thomas and I returned to school specifically to thank Jim for his efforts. I think he appreciated that.

Regards,

Bruce Flood

What an impact and how vast Jim's influence has been, but the reverse can also be true. For every teacher turned off teaching, there can be countless kids turned off learning.

Jimmy Coroneos, although you were lucky enough never to teach me personally, I salute you as an educational Humble Hero.

Editorial comment:
I am occasionally asked to nominate my favourite movie about an inspirational teacher. "Dead Poet's Society", starring Robin Williams and Ethan Hawke, is often put forward as one I am sure to like, and I did, but I didn't love it. I found it a touch over the top, to be honest. Edward James Olmos as Jaimie Escalante in the movie "Stand and Deliver" is more like Mr Coroneos in Dr John's story, but my favourite is Albert Finney in the 1994 movie, "The Browning Version".

Story 46

Keith

Keith, a disenfranchised dad, learns the hard
way that you can't win a kid's heart through the court

$\mathcal{I}$ will remember Keith for the rest of my life because he followed my advice against his better judgement! It must be hard for someone to go to a counsellor with a million things on their mind and accept advice from someone who hardly knows them and is unaware of at least 990,000 of the variables that go into that client's decision-making. I know, as psychologists, we're meant to tease it out and let the client work out a way forward, but Keith and I had done that, and he couldn't move forward.

His wife, Chelsea, was a very loving mum but very protective. Keith and Chelsea had met at a prestigious private school and were the perfect couple, both very well connected. Keith had gone on to university, done a degree in building and an MBA, and was all set to take over the reins from his dad.

But Keith couldn't stand his dad, who used him as his successful showpiece to all his friends. His dad would drive by Keith's mansion, not call in, of course, but tell his friends how successful his son was. Keith had the mansion, the ocean-going yacht, and various other accoutrements that go with wealth; money was no object. Like his dad, Keith tried to win his boys over by showing off and showering them with material things that money can buy – his boys were not impressed. They would rather have lived in a happy home. Chelsea, for her part, was sick and tired of all the posturing and the parties and the loneliness, so they separated. As we all know, money does not buy happiness.

So Chelsea and Keith came to see me to work out the best access arrangements. Things worked out OK for a while, and then, surprise, surprise, Keith found another partner who was far more in awe of his wealth.

As often happens, his new partner, Christine, wanted more of her new love's life. She wasn't keen on his kids wanting all of their dad's time every second weekend, so the access plan faltered.

What had been a civil separation up to then became very uncivil. Chelsea became quite angry, and there's nothing more dangerous than a woman scorned. Chelsea was sick of seeing and hearing about this floozy flaunting her way into the family, their mutual friendships and, as Chelsea saw it, digging ever deeper into the family fortune.

Probably not deliberately, but certainly dangerously, Chelsea decided not to shield the boys from the harsh reality of their father's narcissism. Now the boys were really hurt and came to believe that their dad had duped them over all those years. So when Chelsea asked them if they would like to join her in her move north to Queensland to be nearer to her sister, the boys jumped at the chance to get away from their deceitful dad.

Keith was incensed and had to see me urgently. "How can she do this? I love my boys. I can't let them go! I can and will take her to court and block their move! "

I advised Keith against that stand along the lines that, if he blocked them, that would be just further anti-dad ammunition. The boys would become even more incensed and have nothing to do with him. I advised him to let the family go, smarten up his priorities, keep sending them cards and make regular calls for birthdays, but not to block their move north.

Keith, against his better judgement, reluctantly agreed to accept my advice. I don't know where he and his kids are now, but a few years later, Keith rang to thank me for my help. The kids had started coming back every holiday, and now both boys were back living with him full-time and seeing their mother during holidays.

Two critical lessons were learnt here. Firstly, never sink the other end of the boat, as Chelsea had done, or your end will sink too. Secondly, material trappings mean nothing to kids compared to where your heart is. Both parents learnt a lot, but the damage to the boys could never really be restored.

If you're in a position where a friend or family has really hurt you, anger is an obvious option, just as forgiveness is too. I know a million times over which one is healthier and gets the better outcome.

Editorial comment:
The Mayo Clinic informs me that being hurt by someone, particularly someone you love and trust, can cause anger, sadness and confusion. If you dwell on hurtful events or situations, grudges filled with resentment, vengeance and hostility can take root. If you allow negative feelings to crowd out positive feelings, you might be swallowed up by bitterness or a sense of injustice.

I'm with Dr John on this one. Forgiveness trumps anger every time. "Dumbledore says people find it far easier to forgive others for being wrong than being right."
– J. K. Rowling

Story 47

Noel

Noel, my friend, gives us a lesson in risk
taking and living life to the full while you can

You would have liked Noel, a ginger-haired life-of-the-party guy who never sought self-aggrandisement but just sought fun! From head to toe, Noel was born to laugh and move. He was a great dancer and learnt to play the piano by ear; he couldn't read a note. Everyone thought he was gay, but Noel didn't care. He had a lovely wife, Jeanette and two lovely children.

Noel reminded me very much of that great under-rated Australian singer, composer and songwriter, Peter Allen, of "I Still Call Australia Home" fame. I'm just reading Peter's biography, "The Boy From Oz" by Stephen Maclean. He, too, learnt all his tunes by ear. His biography mentions that great pianist Winifred Atwell made a brief visit to Armidale, where Peter Allen grew up. Peter's mother recalled that after hearing her play at The Capitol, he went straight home and belted out "The Black and White Rag" right through, from start to finish, not a note out of place.

Having lived many years in Armidale, I identified with the Peter Allen story, but he wasn't real for me. Noel was absolutely and authentically real to me for many years.

I first met Noel while teaching in the Riverina in NSW. I was only 19 when we met. He taught in town, and I had my one-teacher school 20 miles out in a rice-growing farming area with 19 kids aged 5 to 14. Back then, our school had no electricity, but I thought it was only proper that my motley crew marched into school the way they did in "big" schools. So I bought some super cool red bongos and would sit on the school verandah and beat out a marching rhythm that would coordinate their footsteps and smarten up any foot draggers.

It worked well, but the bush tom-toms couldn't wait to spread the word about this crazy teacher and his bongos. So the word got to Noel, who had started a band in town. Their drummer had left for saner pastures, and Noel was desperate. Musical talent was sparse in this small town. Noel gave me a call, didn't ask if I could play, didn't ask if I had ever drummed before, just reassured me that I didn't need to worry, to just look the part, and he would cover the beat with his left hand. So we travelled as a band to all the larger towns like Echuca and Swan Hill and Mildura, Victorian border towns, and Noel single-handedly won everyone over. Noel had that magic charisma but more than that, he was prepared to have a go, to trust his arm, make mistakes and learn from them.

Noel and I lost all contact for about 50 years. Eight years ago, out of the blue, Noel called me and asked if he could call in for a chat. He and Jeanette stayed over for the best couple of days ever. You know with true friends, how the years melt away. But his news wasn't good. He had an aggressive form of prostate cancer, and although he was prepared to line up for even the experimental drugs, the prognosis wasn't favourable. We caught up several times in the next few years, and each time we'd be around the piano, bursting into whatever took our fancy, especially gospel music.

Just before Noel died a few years ago, we went to see him, and he still staggered out of bed and indulged my wish to sing a few more gospel songs together. We loved belting out that old favourite, "The Old Rugged Cross". I can still hear us hamming it up for all it was worth, "On a hill far away stood an old rugged cross, the emblem of suffering and shame".

I was privileged to say a few words at his packed funeral service. But Noel taught me so much about chancing my arm, giving it a go, making choices that energised the soul, and being prepared to make mistakes. I so miss Noel, but what a wonderful legacy he left. Hopefully, that legacy will rub off on you too. Noel had no great faith or expectation of where he was headed in the afterlife, but wherever he is, even in my soul, Noel is making music!

I just had this very belated thought. If he and Peter Allen ever catch up, oh boy!

Noel, you'll do me as a Humble Hero any and every day of the week!

Editorial comment:
Dr John suggested that I look up this poem. It's a reminder that mental risks are part of healthy homes. For those who are over-fearful, the first risk is to admit that feeling, the second risk is to share it and then the big risk, doing something about it, has already been conquered –
> *To laugh is to risk appearing the fool.*
> *To weep is to risk appearing sentimental.*
> *To reach out is to risk involvement.*
> *To expose feelings is to risk exposing your true self.*
> *To place your ideas and dreams before the crowd is to risk their love.*
> *To love is to risk not being loved in return.*
> *To live is to risk dying.*
> *To hope is to risk despair.*
> *To try is to risk failure.*
> *But the greatest hazard in life is to risk nothing.*
> *The one who risks nothing does nothing and has nothing –*
> *and finally is nothing.*
> *He may avoid suffering and sorrow,*
> *But he simply cannot learn, feel, change, grow or love.*
> *Chained by this certitude, he is a slave; he has forfeited freedom.*
> *Only one who risks is free!*
> *– William Arthur Ward*

Story 48

Jonathan

The "boy in the bubble" gives us all a lesson in
inspirational leadership

Here's part of a special poem, simply called "It's Too Much to Hope For", written by an extraordinary person.

> It's too much to hope for a life without pain. It's wrong to expect a life without pain, for pain is our body's defense. No matter how much we dislike it.
>
> Pain is important, and for pain we should be grateful! How else would we know…
>
> To move our hand from the fire? Our finger from the blade? Our foot from the thorn?
>
> So pain is important, and for pain we should be grateful!
>
> Yet, there's a type of pain that serves no purpose, that's chronic pain.
>
> It's that elite band of pain that's not for defense. It's an attacking force. An attacker from within,
>
> A destroyer of personal happiness, an aggressive assailant on personal ability,
>
> A ceaseless invader of personal peace and a continuous harassment to life!
>
> Chronic pain is the hardest hurdle for the mind to jump, sometimes it is almost impossible to jump. Yet, we must keep trying, and trying, and trying,
>
> Because if we don't, it will destroy.
>
> And the mind can manage it and the mind will become stronger for the practice!

Wow, all pretty deep and insightful, eh? What if I tell you it was written by a nine-year-old boy who lived daily with chronic pain – you'd probably say incredible and inspirational. But wait, there's more.

Over the last few years, the teenager Greta Thunberg has been attracting worldwide media attention for her stance on climate change. Still, the same boy who wrote that poem, Jonathan Wilson-Fuller, the Boy in the

Bubble, over 30 years ago was already in print with his incredible climate change warning in his book, "Will You Please Listen: I Have Something to Say". Jonathan's sensitivities made him virtually "our canary down the mines," warning us of the peril of our ways.

Jonathan was given the "Boy in the Bubble" label because he was allergic to the environment. I met him when I was a regular on the Channel Nine Breakfast "Today" show – he was 11 years old. The Producer asked if I could interview Jonathan for a segment on TV.

What an experience. Jonathan wore a mask and protective clothing, and I couldn't use any deodorant, no aftershave, no aromas of any sort. Then we arrived at the house for filming. After our gear got the all-clear we were escorted to the lounge room and Jonathan was carried in to meet us, very pale and wan but what a brilliant and incisive mind.

Even at that tender age, Jonathan was doing Year 12 Maths and Science. His message was clear way back then. Why don't people listen? We are polluting our planet, sending waste into our oceans and carbon dioxide into the atmosphere.

We might say, "But what can one individual do about it?" Jonathan said, "We might just be one little drop in the ocean, but it's those drops that make the ocean – if we all unite across the world in demanding change, we could turn the tide, we could swamp the world with our message."

Thirty years ago, Jonathan was shouting this message. If an 11-year-old could see it, is it just apathy or greed making it much harder for adults?

Jonathan, my Humble Heroes' collection wouldn't be complete without you. Even to this day, I regard you as one of my most inspirational teachers of all time. Thank you!

Editorial comment:
I love that quote from Jonathan, "We might just be one little drop in the ocean, but it's those drops that make the ocean – if we all unite across the world in demanding change, we could turn the tide, we could swamp the world with our message."

It reminds me of that "feel-good" song from 1970 sung by The Brotherhood of Man.
"For united we stand
Divided we fall
And if our backs should ever be against the wall
We'll be together, together, you and I"
– Goodison and Hiller

Story 49

Matthew

Seven-year-old Matthew turns the tables on his father

(a retired Major no less) in a lesson on listening

$\mathcal{I}$f you have a child in your family who never listens, then you'll be right on side with Tracey. Tracey was the mother of a perfectly behaved five-year-old daughter, Patrice, and a parent-deaf seven-year-old, Matthew.

This family would drive hundreds of kilometres to see me about their problem son, who just wouldn't listen, and it was driving his dad mad.

Matthew had to be told a dozen times to do something by mum before he cooperated, and then it was only after she screamed, "Matthew do as you're told!" so loudly that dad would go dotty in his den. You see, dad was an older-than-average dad, a retired army Major who had remarried to a much younger lady and now ran a consultancy from his home office.

However, the fact that the Major had to listen to it all while his son blissfully blocked out mum's "Matthews" was more than the Major could manage. Of course, there was the alternative that he back mum up with firm love but bringing up the kids was not men's work.

Meanwhile, pencils were snapping in his office, and his Johnny Walker tonic was just not working as the Major became increasingly flustered by Matthew's "insubordination", as he called it.

Home habits are hard to break, but everyone was unhappy with how it was, so they each agreed to change one horrible habit about themselves. Matthew had to listen to what he was told. Mum was to stop telling him more than once. Dad's was to back mum up rather than back out. Young Patrice had to change the habit of asking mum to return for another goodnight kiss.

So they used a chart to record every time Matthew heard mum the first time. Mum deliberately let him miss out on a few things when he didn't listen the first time. If listening was a priority, then dad's job was to give Matthew some listening practice. This was done at electronic device-playing time. Dad had to call Matthew's name, followed by some instructions. Matthew hated it, but his listening did improve.

However, as dad started to take a bit more interest in his little listening lout, he noticed that Matthew never missed a whisper or hearing the word "ice cream" no matter where he was in the house. So to expedite the progress and show how clever he was, the Major started calling him

"Ice Cream". "Excuse me, Ice Cream, can you come for dinner now?" Young Matthew was furious. "Don't call me that," he moaned. "My name is Matthew. "

It's a lovely story and shows it is possible to change home habits, but there was a sting in this case. A tearful Matthew told mum at bedtime one evening that dad never listened to him! Dad was always too busy in his den. Tracey thought about it and devised a brilliant plan to help out. They both agreed on this, and Matthew became a much better listener overnight.

Anytime Matthew couldn't get the Major's attention, Tracey suggested that he call out "Johnny Walker," which got dad's attention every time. The Major was not amused.

Like every family, they're hanging in there. They have their good and bad days, but they're a family.

To all the parents and grandparents putting up with parent-deaf kids, today you get my Humble Heroes' Award for sheer patience.

Editorial comment:
That story was exhausting, Dr John. What are the rewards for parents and grandparents who demonstrate patience daily in their caring roles? From the famous marshmallow experiments at Stanford in the 70s, we know that delayed gratification benefits children in later life. As carers, we must permit ourselves to find patience by dialling down the stress. Carers need ways to take care of themselves so they aren't at the stress level of blowing their top every day.

" Kids don't want cool parents. They want parents that keep their cool. "
– Hal Runkel

Story 50

Pat

Magistrate Pat O'Shane has some salutary words
for parents and their responsibility to provide
boundaries for their kids

Celebrity Contribution

*M*any Australian readers, particularly those in New South Wales, will know and respect the name Pat O'Shane.

Pat O'Shane has been a well-known and respected Children's Magistrate and has always been very proud of her Aboriginal heritage. Pat was kind enough to contribute to my book "Who'd Be a Parent" some years ago, and I found her story so powerful I've included an excerpt here.

> *I see so many parents today who seem to be afraid of their children, afraid that if they take a stand, they won't be popular. But in my view, I'm the parent and being a parent carried very clear and important responsibilities.*
>
> *I had no hesitation in making it clear to the children that I was in charge. This was my house, my rules and my consequences. They didn't always like it, but as they've grown up — they've told me that they respected me for it.*
>
> *A good example of how we operated as a family was this experience with my daughter when she was doing her HSC. They had an end-of-term party, and I'd always said, "Never get into the car with a driver who has had anything to drink. Call me if you need, any time, day or night and I'll come and get you but don't get in that car."*
>
> *This night I got a call about 2am, and I went to the party — and took her home, and she was fine. That same night her friends got into the car with a driver who had been drinking, and several were killed. True story!*
>
> *That upset my daughter enormously for a long time, but I think it also brought home the message — that I had a reason for taking the strong lines that I did from time to time.*
>
> *You have to learn to say "No", and that is sometimes very hard.*
>
> *I subscribe to the view that there's too much emphasis on children's rights without an equal emphasis on their responsibilities too — and that includes housework.*
>
> *I think it's about time we stood up and put some of these parenting responsibilities back on the agenda.*
>
> *In the children's court a little while ago, there was a young lady before*

us, and she was, in my judgement and from my experience, a wilful miss!

Her solicitors were pleading for light treatment but I felt she was just being wilful and needed firm management and ruled accordingly.

Her solicitors were shocked and horrified.

I said to them, "Not only have I sat on thousands of cases such as these, not only am I a parent myself, but I've also taught thousands of children – that is my judgement from my experience, and that is my ruling."
Sure we must treat children with respect, but they also have to learn how to earn that respect. It all comes back to parental responsibility.

There is nothing more important or more urgent than that in today's families.

Wow. I just love firm straightforward parenting. Who else can if we can't give the lead in our children's lives?

Pat O'Shane, for speaking up and speaking out for so many years for the welfare of Australia's most important asset, our children, I welcome you to the Humble Heroes' Hall of Fame!

Editorial comment:
Wow, indeed. There's a lot of tough love on show in this story. Tough love is all right, but some would argue it has nothing to do with love. Jan Hunt, the Director of the Natural Child Project, believes that to love a child means treating them with respect, patience, gentleness and compassion, and in a way consistent with the Golden Rule.

"What kind of love is it if it doesn't allow for mistakes (which all of us make)?"
– Jan Hunt

Series 6

Elizabeth Jean

Elizabeth (aka Jean) shows so much compassion and love for children with severe disabilities, I end up marrying her

Elizabeth (she hated that name) was working with moderately intellectually delayed children when I first met her.

At that stage, I was the School Counsellor for the school where Elizabeth was the Head Teacher. She asked me to give a sex talk to the boys, as a few of the bigger boys had been trying to use the safety scissors to cut off a younger boy's penis!

After that, I became very interested in Elizabeth's work and absolutely in awe of how she handled those children.

I recall one visit when Elizabeth washed down one of the teenage Down's Syndrome boys after he had soiled himself.

Her washing caused Jimmy to have an erection, and Elizabeth looked to Jenny, her off-sider, as to what she should do. Jenny was calling out, "Hit it with a pencil, hit it with a pencil," signalling that Jenny had previous experience with this problem – in her professional or personal life. All the children and Jenny were goggle-eyed, watching from behind the glass.

But it was Elizabeth's work in the Christmas concerts that had me in awe and in stitches. The children had been practising the scene where the boy and girl fall asleep on stage next to a chimney. Then Santa comes in with presents in his sack and leaves them beside the chimney while the children sleep.

The children knew what to do, but there hadn't been a dress rehearsal, well, not with the beard. Santa had a beard as well as a bag and presents. As he held the bag with his right hand and reached into the bag with his left, the beard dropped into the bag.

Here was the dilemma. Santa used his left hand to hold his beard back in place. But then there was no hand left to get the presents out! Once again, Santa used his left hand to keep the beard out; again, there was no hand to take out the presents. Santa tentatively let go of the beard to remove the gifts, but the same problem occurred.

This routine occurred seven or eight times. Meanwhile, the children were getting impatient and calling out unscripted comments. "Hurry up, Santa!" But Santa had no answers.

Quietly and efficiently, Elizabeth came on stage and held Santa's beard so he could finish his routine.

Everything Elizabeth did with those children, and every child she worked with, including her own three girls, was done with the same love and belief in their goodness that she showed that day.

I couldn't believe that any teacher could always find a good core in every child, no matter how difficult the problem or behaviour was.

I was so influenced by Elizabeth's capacity for love and her capabilities with every child she met that I ended up marrying her!

Fifty-four years later, we are still married, and every day, I am in awe of that wonderful lady – and in fear of that pencil!

{ *Editorial comment:*
A sweet story, Dr John. It's a touching and moving story. What a
wonderful way to say "Thank you" to your partner of fifty-four years.
So much better than a card or a bunch of flowers. }

Story 52

Graham

Graham was school phobic but dad came up with some electronic magic to zap him out of it – and I was the beneficiary

*L*ook around your house, and you've probably got photos, cards or gifts that someone you love and remember has given to you. Because I worked for so long with so many kids, I have accumulated a few myself.

Let me share my time with Graham and his gift to me. Graham was a boy whose IQ far exceeded his EQ (Emotional Intelligence), so school was hell for him. Like many school-phobic kids, he was very bright but sensitive and not very good socially.

Mum was a very busy and successful artist – Dad was an engineer but couldn't cope with bureaucratic pressures, so he became an odd-job handyman. But just normal financial pressures meant mum had to work long and hard and attend exhibitions and was very preoccupied.

Somewhere in there, Graham got lost. He hated leaving home because he was a real mum's boy, and mum was emotionally distant. His phobia had a double whammy – he hated the bullying and teasing he got at school, particularly from Branco, because he was a "nerd".

The absentee notes started to pile up as Graham used every excuse to avoid school. As an ex-teacher, I used to love some of the reasons parents gave for their children's absence. Just because I love the humour, here are a few I saved.

> "Please excuse Natalie as her father was home."

> "Please excuse Paul for whichever day he was away last week."

> "Sorry, Mick wasn't at school. Couldn't move the mongrel!"

And what about this one?

> "Please excuse Paul for being. It was his father's fault."

Back to Graham – it got to the point that he wouldn't even leave the house. He spent his days curled up on his bed in the foetal position, locking himself away from life. I remember one particular incident as if it were yesterday. Graham tried to hang himself from the shower curtain rail when he was teased and bullied by Branco. Fortunately, the shower rail was flimsy and collapsed before it had done him damage.

His family was devastated. Mum cut out after-school art commitments, and dad spent more time doing electronic "stuff" with Graham.

We had a session with the teacher, got some medication into the mix, involved the School Counsellor, and had a supportive action plan.

If kids have something to live for and to love, then every family has a way to win success. In Graham's case, that lifeline was his electronics.

The school put Branco, the bully, on notice that kindness was the key to him continuing at the school, and they even used our beloved WorryWoos with him. Graham's dad helped him develop an electronic kit. Dad rewarded him with $2 for each new back-to-school goal he achieved, like getting out of the house, going past the school, going through the school grounds after hours, going to the computer room during hours and so on.

An ecstatic Graham phoned me a few weeks later to tell me he'd made it to school. The long-term outcome was that Graham survived school, albeit with grades that didn't reflect his IQ, and he's now a young man working in Sydney with an IT company.

And why am I so proud? When this poor kid could not make it out of the house, he made me a laser detector to tell me when my teenage daughters were back in!

Editorial comment:
That's a lovely positive story, Dr John. I love a happy ending. Tony Robbins tells his readers that anyone who has achieved something worthwhile has had challenges and setbacks – because anything worth doing will be difficult. Overcoming adversity is a necessary step on the road to greatness.

"He that wrestles with us strengthens our nerves and sharpens our skill. Our antagonist is our helper."
– Edmund Burke

Story 53

Lisa

Lisa is suffering from a different form of PTSD
Post Teen Stress Disorder – and is still living proof
that if you hang in there, love wins through

*F*or those readers with teenagers and those who have suffered the other "PTSD" ("Post Teen Stress Disorder"), or have vivid memories, then this story is for you. Lisa and Dean had five boys! Lisa was a talented no-nonsense schoolteacher, and Dean was a fairly compliant builder.

You can't have five boys and not have problems as they move from dependence to independence or, as some comic described it, the move from "infancy to adultery".

Stephen, their eldest, was a bit of a rebel; as he got older, he hung out with a rebellious group. Fortunately, his dad was heavily involved in Rugby League, so all the boys at least learnt the rules and played the game. But the teen years for Lisa were very demanding as she felt she had to be mum and dad to all six messy males.

However, Stephen's problems came to a head one Saturday night when the police called Lisa at 1am to say Stephen had been involved in a bit of a skirmish. He had bad-mouthed the police trying to restore calm, so he'd been locked up for a while – would she come and get him? You can imagine mum's mood.

When Lisa got to the police station, she apologised profusely for Stephen's behaviour, and they let him go with a formal caution. Stephen asked if mum could also drop his mate Leon home. Lisa obliged, but the trip home was not pleasant. Lisa was seething in the front, and the boys were bad-mouthing the police in the back – saying "the pigs had it in for us", "discrimination", "bullying", and other clichés.

Halfway home, Lisa could stand it no more. Still seething, she pulled off the road, slammed to a halt and, between gritted teeth, offered these prophetic words to both boys. "Right, I'm going to put you both straight in five words. Life sucks – cop it sweet!"

Then Lisa drove home with nobody saying a word. That didn't fix the problem, however, and as soon as school was over, Stephen high-tailed it up to Schoolies on the Gold Coast and sent his mum a message saying he'd met some mates and was going to flat with them.

Fortunately, his parents didn't succumb to his messages along the lines of, "Hi mum, no mon, send some. " Stephen had to get money somewhere to support his habit, and although his lifestyle precluded him from being a great footy player, he was a terrific ref. As a Junior Ref, Stephen was considered fair, knowledgeable, and a no-nonsense young man. Stephen was not even ruffled by that nasty group of humans, euphemistically called "parent supporters", who use the sidelines to vent their spleen about everyone except their team. Refs were in high demand up in Queensland so that Queensland could retain ownership of the State of Origin!

Stephen joined the Ref's Association to get work. A couple of older guys could see that Stephen was pretty mixed up but a good kid, so they took him under their wing, backed his application to referee and even went further. One of them found work for Stephen as an apprentice roof-tiler.

With similar skills to his dad, Stephen blitzed it, met a girl, moved out into his own apartment, and now has two kids. He even deigns to come down and visit the oldies to put his brothers straight!

It's not easy being the sole female in an all-male household. Mind you, Lisa could match them and give as good as she got. When the family had "an altercation", the language that flowed "would make a bullocky blush," Lisa quipped to me one day during a tirade about her messy males, "If they flop on the lounge, dominate the devices, flog the fridge and leave you all the cleaning up – then you either married them or gave birth to them."

As a postscript to this story, once the boys all had jobs, and I suppose to escape her life of servitude, Lisa and Dean took off in their van. They're somewhere around Australia, but for some reason, they're not easy to contact.

Editorial comment:
Five boys living in the same household. That's a challenge, for sure. Teach them early how to clean the toilet – that's my advice! Maggie Dent, the author of "From Boys to Men", suggests that with constant, warm guidance and correction and bucketloads of patience, little boys can get better at making decisions that cause their parents less frustration and stress. She also advises Mums to keep "a hidden supply of good chocolate too and know that you may need more coffee."

Story 54

Mr Hanky

Mr Hanky is used to great effect to
solve Karl's bowel problems

Something that works wonders with kids, far better than bribes, threats, lectures or logic, is to use their imagination! Just look at how powerful concepts like Santa, Easter Bunny and Tooth Fairy are, for instance. And just look at how children bring to life inanimate objects like their teddies and dolls and how petrified they can become as they animate shadows and night noises that become monsters and burglars.

For years now, I've had lots of success fighting these imaginary fears, not with adult logic but in a fun way, creating other fictitious characters or scenes to knock out these night-time nasties.

But Karl had me beaten. One of the perennial problems with many young kids is soiling! Sometimes it's because of past pain in passing stools, an anal fissure, fear of losing part of their body, or for no apparent reason whatsoever. Some will only do it in their nappies, some hang on for days, and some have to squat in a particular spot. The real worries are those who become petrified about doing poos and get constipated.

Once that happens, not only do they become unwell, but the distended anal muscles often cannot stop little bits of their stools from sneaking through – "sneaky poos", we call it.

Under normal circumstances, I'd be working intensely on a remedy – establishing regular toilet routine, ensuring their diet was strong in fibre and fruit juices to stimulate the kidneys and having some particular activity they can only do when they're on the loo (like reading a specific book). Karl wasn't responding.

Then some older kids told me about Mr Hanky in the TV comedy "South Park", supposedly made for kids. In this particular episode, the kid community had been deprived of all the Christmas symbols because some minority groups took exception. So, as kids must have imagination in their lives, they ended up animating a stool or "poo" and called it Mr Hanky!

This gave me the idea to help Karl! I told him about poor Mr Hanky, who was every kid's friend, but suggested that Mr Hanky stank because he hated being squashed in nappies. What Mr Hanky loved was to swim and dive. So when Karl's tummy started grumbling, Mr Hanky was telling him that he was ready to go for his swim.

Better still, Mr Hanky loved to dive too, so if Karl wanted to be kind to

Mr Hanky, he just pushed with his tummy muscles and plopped Mr Hanky into the water he loved. Then when Karl finished depositing team Hanky, they just flushed the toilet and Mr Hanky could then swim right out to sea where all his mates' poos (his mates were all toilet trained) were having a great "poo" party. Karl loved the idea and responded – it took all the anger and conflict out of toileting and made it much more fun.

I will never forget not just the delight on Karl's face but the look of absolute disbelief on mum's face! I'm sure she was bemused beyond belief that she was paying for this insane, in-anal treatment of Karl's condition.

Of course, you have to be careful how you word it. One mum told me she failed to specify that it was loo water they loved! Her young fella dropped it in the bath and was having great fun playing and chatting to Mr Hanky and all his friends!

Long live, Mr Hanky!!

Editorial comment:
My wife was better able to appreciate this story than I was. In her role as Nana, she is closer to the action than I am. Many toilet training methods I have come across involve rewards or distractions. The Montessori method intrigues me as it is an entirely different approach.

"There should be no pressure, no reward or punishment, no adult deciding when the child should learn to use the potty. The environment is prepared and the child is free to explore and imitate in these natural developmental stages."
–The Joyful Child

Story 55

Mothers

A tribute to the unconditional love of mothers
and a huge thank you on behalf of the rest of us

$\mathcal{I}$'m sure you knew the faults of your mum but loved her nevertheless for all the sacrifices made to give us a start. I will never stop praising my mum or any mum – for those long hard yards everyone has put in. This is almost universal regardless of their pain, loneliness, sadness, feelings of not being needed anymore – even their failings and frailties.

Having three daughters constantly reminds me of the never-ending workload mothers are expected to cover – the housework, spouse work, kids' work, homework, and earning an income to help with the mortgage.

Furthermore, as one in two marriages now end in divorce, even if the partner is generous and fair, the day-to-day logistics of ferrying the kids to school, ballet, sport, cheerleading, music practice etc., are generally done by mum, who has to surrender income-producing hours to do this. Small wonder that single Mums are so highly represented in the poverty statistics. I can only think back to one couple where, after the divorce, mum played hardball and just dumped the kids at dad's whether he was home or not. It was his turn, and it was up to him to work it out. Is that tough love or just tough?

Having said all the above, I'm sure many women would have reneged had they known what lay in store. I'm reminded of some of the genuine and heartfelt stories in Carolyne Lee and Susan Burke's now out-of-print book, "Who'd Be a Mother". In the book, Carolyne Lee puts her feelings about the experience of motherhood this way.

> I find it hard to admit this – but my reasons for choosing to have a baby were not thought out – or even realistic. Back then – I saw pregnancy, childbirth, breastfeeding and caring for a small child as essentially sensuous – enriching experiences that I wanted to have for myself.

> It simply never occurred to me that the act of creation – particularly of a new life – is all about giving and giving and giving.

> But babies are good teachers – mine quickly showed the destructiveness of all my selfish and self-centred notions. It was a painful time, and the learning process is probably still unfinished.

As a mere male, I emerge from such testimonies with the feeling that those who have been there have an understanding and feeling for humanity that the rest of us can never quite grasp. And when you think about it, who in their right mind would lightly take on the mantle of motherhood?

Look how the Job Description reads:

WANTED - MOTHER

Hours of work

24 hours by 24 years, so pace yourself and find space for yourself.

Holidays

Nil – so be selfish, two weeks in a caravan mightn't suit – short trips, decent breaks or swapped roles might.

Qualifications

The University of you-name-it expected, so in-service training through friends, family, social media, Playgroup, kids' clinic, magazines and telephone is essential.

Salary

Costed at $2000 + per week, so don't settle for just free board and beggings.

Travel

Plenty of travel opportunities – mainly to school, after school activities and supermarket, so make sure you have easy means of getting to shops, parks and friends.

Promotion

Nil - so be careful not to achieve through your kids and find some areas that give personal satisfaction.

Tenure

Permanent – so don't panic over a few mistakes.

Maybe next Mother's Day you could advertise the job at home and if you're selected, put your conditions in writing and mean it.

To all the Mums, whatever your age or imperfections or infirmity –

Thank you.

Editorial comment:
I love the humour in this story. The Polar explorer Ernest Shackleton is said to have advertised for prospective expeditioners in the London Times with this advert.
"Men wanted for hazardous journey; small wages, bitter cold, long months of complete darkness, constant danger, safe return doubtful. Honour and recognition in case of success."
Apparently he was inundated with responses.
According to one advertising executive –
"Motherhood is like that heroic age of Antarctic exploration; it is a heroic expedition that, despite their better judgement, people embark on all the time."
– Nick Kelly, Irish Times

Story 56

Trevor

Trevor goes the extra mile in trying to win over
his step-son – and has to become a
superhero to do it

When she met Trevor, Natalie was separated with one seven-year-old son, Mark. Trevor was a mechanic with four daughters to rear on his own after his wife died following a long battle with depression.

When I met them, they were a blended family – Natalie got on well with Trevor's girls, and although they went through some tough teenage years, the family was holding together. Not so Mark, who felt he was the outsider in a family of girls. He missed his dad and didn't get on well with Trevor, whom he saw as stealing his mum. Everything suggested that the discord between the two was mutual.

But Natalie was adamant in demanding that Trevor get a better relationship going with Mark, or they couldn't marry. Trevor, Mark and I worked on sharing some home truths about feeling rejected, about the loss of a loved one and about lack of respect. Trevor agreed to put in some long and hard yards to try and get a good relationship going with Mark as he really wanted to marry Natalie.

Putting in hard yards, in this case, meant Trevor calling on his own dad, a retired mechanic, to come back into the shop and help out. Trevor's dad came in two afternoons a week and Saturday morning so Trevor could take Mark to his much-loved soccer practice and the Saturday game. Trevor got on well with the coach, became the half-time orange supplier, and took his turn washing the shirts. In time the genuine commitment of Trevor to Mark paid off, and they became much better friends.

But Mark still didn't want this wedding thing to happen and said he wouldn't go. Trevor now had a dilemma. Natalie was keen, and the girls were excited, but the whole thing soured over Mark. I don't know how and when he did it, but on their way home from soccer training, Trevor stopped the car and asked Mark what he could do to make this wedding thing work. They agreed, and to this day, I don't know whether Mark was testing Trevor or making him do penance, but the next time I saw them was after the wedding. They brought along some photos, and honest to God, there was Mark in a Superman suit and Trevor dressed in a Superman suit too!

Natalie must have swallowed a lot of pride to marry that Superman! This all happened a few years ago, and Mark is now an apprentice mechanic in

Trevor's garage, and they get on well. When I mention the cape caper, they both just look sheepishly away and smile.

Sometimes I think I've made sacrifices for my kids, but Mark and Trevor taught me a massive lesson in sacrificial love! Trevor, you're now in my Hall of Fame, not just as a Humble Hero but as a super-Humble Hero!

Editorial comment:
Some of us include the concept of sacrifice in our definition of what it means to truly love another person. Research shows that couples are happier and more likely to remain in their relationships if they are willing to sacrifice for each other. Many believe their religion is in part founded on sacrifice.

Story 57

Dr Steve

Doctors need to be highly sensitive re the power
imbalance between doctor and patient, as I learn
the hard way!

Have you ever played a practical joke on someone and had it come back to "bite you on the bum", as they say? Dr Steve was a bit of a hero for me and significantly influenced my practice in more ways than one!

Some years ago, when I was a lecturer in Armidale, I developed quite a taste for Australian red wines. Indeed, some classy cool-climate reds are now being grown in that area. Occasionally my friend Stan and I would toddle along to the odd wine tasting and, of course, met quite a few of the locals, including our surgeon friend, Dr Steve.

Now Steve fancied himself as a wine connoisseur, and I thought he was a tad pretentious about it all. One time Stan and I bought a bottle of the "Chocolate Shop: Red wine with dark chocolate flavouring". I suppose intended for those who prefer a sweeter taste. I couldn't help myself. We caught up with Dr Steve and offered him a taste. He had one taste, put his glass back down on the table with some gusto and proudly announced that, in his opinion, there was a hint of chocolate. After leading him along, I showed him the bottle with "chocolate flavouring" on the label. Dr Steve was not amused, but we all had a good laugh, and we remained friends.

Sometime later, I was diagnosed with a medical condition requiring a colonoscopy. Without hesitation, I asked for the referral to nominate my friend Dr Steve.

As you may know, they do these procedures in day surgery, and they had me booked in first. I was out of the theatre and back in the day surgery recovery ward by 11am and feeling fine.

Other patients were wheeled in after their "procedure" until the room was full of patients in varying stages of recovery.

In the afternoon, after the procedures were complete, Dr Steve, still in his operating garb, came in accompanied by a nurse with her clipboard of patient notes.

Although I had been "done" first, Dr Steve deliberately avoided eye contact or coming anywhere near my bed. He went around the room to share good news, but he asked a few patients to see him in a fortnight in his rooms.

I waited and waited and became increasingly anxious and frightened as to what my diagnosis and prognosis would be.

Eventually, with everyone else dealt with and many dressed and moved out, Dr Steve came to me. At that point, Steve turned to the nurse, told her she could go now and drew the blue curtains around my bed.

This was it, I thought. Steve came up to the bedside and, in a subdued voice and serious face, said, "John, I didn't want to say anything in front of all the people here. They don't need to know our penchant for good wine, but I heard you mention at the tasting the other day, that you can get hold of some Hill of Grace. I love that wine, but I can't find it in any of the catalogues. I was wondering whether you could get a couple of bottles for me. Oh, by the way, the colonoscopy was fine. I just took off a couple of polyps, but everything looks good. "

I could have killed him on the spot, but the reality was that I was so relieved, all I could do was shout loud enough for anyone outside the curtain to wonder about the propriety of it all, "Yes, Steve, no worries, of course, I'll get you a couple!" Dr Steve then thanked me politely and shuffled on in his moon boots but with a lift in his stride and a grin, or was it a smirk on his face? Was he just getting even with me over the chocolate incident, or was he unaware of how much damage that white coat and the operating garb can do to patients?

I can promise you, from that point on, I have always been so super conscious of the client's fears and trepidations and the incredible power imbalance between doctor and patient. Furthermore, I've learnt not to mess with the guy with the scalpel or the woman with the rolling pin. Big lessons learnt!

Editorial comment:
I'm sure many readers can relate to that story. Feeling powerless is one of the worst side effects of coping with a medical condition. In the final analysis, however, as Dr John illustrates time after time, laughter is often the best medicine.

Story 58

The Plover

Research into animal behaviour
and parenting styles has much to teach us

*M*y Humble Hero for this story is the much-despised plover or masked lapwing!

Here's why. We live near water, and I've been fascinated by how seagulls and plovers rear their children.

When the young gull goes somewhere it shouldn't, mum and dad sit up in our gutter and squawk at the young one to move to safety, but give no directions or help. As a result, the young ones run frantically every which way in panic.

The plovers, by contrast, with outstretched wings, will guide the fledgling to where it should go and, if it is in danger, will bravely confront the enemy with both wings outstretched to make it look fierce.

But they're not the only ones to have trouble parenting. An extract from a "New Scientist" article grabbed my attention.

> The little ones, fighting for their mothers' attention, went into a massive convulsion, literally throwing a fit, throwing themselves at their mothers' feet, beating, even bashing themselves and banging their heads.

If this sounds like your little chicken, rest easy, it's the recorded behaviour of a pelican chicken.

By contrast, in the budgie world, the mothers stand for no tantrums. They feed according to a strict roster based on age but not size, and the fathers are a soft touch.

As a result, the chicks are orderly when mum's in charge and chaos reigns when dad drops in.

The author of the "New Scientist" article draws the following inference about these odd parenting proclivities. "Why the male has never been able to evolve an effective strategy against manipulation remains a mystery, though the infrequency with which he feeds the young is one likely reason. " Heh, does that ring a bell?

Here's another interesting observation. Researchers have found that monkey mothers and infants living in captivity displayed a much lower level of conflict than any other monkey species studied in the wild.

The explanation they give is that in the wild, the conflict occurred because mum was so busy trying to earn her crust. She didn't have enough time to attend to the kids, so they pestered, fought, argued, and performed until they forced her to notice them.

But in captivity, mum didn't have to spend as much time finding food so she could play with the kids, so they were more settled.

In other words, Mums with a bit more spare time had less trouble with the kids.

There was one exception to this rule. When a male came on the scene, and mating was in the wind, the little ones got the cold shoulder. Wild or enclosed, it didn't matter. The kids played up – and no jellybeans or M&Ms tossed out the bedroom door could have silenced them.

So why should reflections like these be in a book about memories? I believe the pace at which we rear kids now, the hours we work and the time the kids spend on electronic devices are causing a problem. American researchers call it "increasing disengagement with our children"– and we will pay a high price for that long-term.

Among all the hard-earned money for devices and toys for kids, I'd have to say that the best thing you can spend on your kids is your time!

Editorial comment:
My experience informs me that parental stress dramatically impacts children's ability to settle into school. Overlay health and housing issues, everything else that was going on before the Covid-19 crisis happened, and the compounding challenges can make it impossible to prioritise education.

"Some students still go to school because it's a safe space. But if they're tired, hungry, or unable to concentrate because they're worried about their family's circumstances, they fail to engage, and their attendance drops off, especially for older students."
– Colleen, Family Partnership Coordinator, Smith Family

Story 59

Damien

Damien's family struck tragedy but it was
the positive outlook of Damien that started
their road to recovery

How does your family go about solving its problems? Some pretend they don't have any, and some, like me, go for the quick solution and back onto the happy stuff.

Some live as if life is just one big problem on the way to the grave – others opt for something to pop, sniff, drink or jab to take away the pain and the problem.

But let me tell you about Jaclyn, a lady who has had her share of problems. The husband had an alcohol problem and walked in front of a bus. Jaclyn sought refuge in the Church and ended up marrying the Minister, Charles, who was also a widower with three young children.

However, Jaclyn couldn't cope with Charles' dogmatic style, so the marriage fell through over time, but Charles' three kids begged to stay with Jaclyn, so they did. Charles would have them over to his place one night during the week as his weekends were tied up with Church.

In amongst all this, Jaclyn's son, Greg, her stalwart and her rock, left school, became an apprentice electrician and loved it. Jaclyn was so proud of him. However, as fate would have it, Greg was electrocuted on the job. Jaclyn struggled with three young boys, a hijacked heart, and a massive mortgage. Life was too much.

I was working with her six-year-old son, Damien, through the school. He was sad like the rest of the family, so I introduced him to Wince the WorryWoo. I read the accompanying Andi Green book, "Don't Feed the Worry Bug", and Damien agreed that the family might have listened too much to the worry bug. The worry bug was getting bigger and bigger, and their confidence as a family was shrinking.

We started our little campaign to beat that worry bug, like saying, "Go away, worry bug, you're just trying to make everyone sad. I can beat you!" They put Wince and the worry bug on the shelf in the living room to remind them of their battle.

Just recently, mum told me about their big breakthrough – when Jaclyn was at one of her lowest points in the morning and not making very good contact with her kids, Damien asked her what was wrong.

Jaclyn curtly reminded him of why she was so sad, and then Damien came through with such simple kid logic. He blurted out "Well, mum, what are we going to do about it? Why don't we see what problems we can solve today and who can solve them the best?"

Just an innocent comment, but it turned Jaclyn's life around. Instead of avoiding problems and living in fear that there'd be more, Jaclyn led by example – they confronted their fears and worries.

Each morning over a hurried breakfast, the family would rattle off what problems they expected or feared that day (e. g. that no one would play with them), and then in the evening, they'd talk about how they solved that problem or whether the thing they feared just didn't happen.

In other words, they confronted their fears and accepted that problems were part of life. Most problems come to "pass", and for those problems that don't go away, the secret is finding ways to solve them – and celebrating their power over the worry bug.

There you go! Swap a problem. It's always easier to solve someone else's!

Editorial comment:
The experts tell us not to fear fear! Sometimes that is easier said than done.

The Child Mind Institute's Elianna Platt tells us:
"Being afraid sometimes is a normal, healthy part of growing up. " While kids do unfortunately sometimes face things that are truly frightening, most garden-variety childhood fears don't represent an actual threat — the "monster" in the closet is just an old coat you've been meaning to donate — which means they actually present an ideal chance for kids to work on their self-regulation skills. But for that to happen, parents often have to address their own anxiety first. – Rae Jacobson, Child Mind Institute

Janine

Janine Shepherd talks about her tragic
accident and her mental, physical and
spiritual fight back to represent Australia

Celebrity Contribution

In the Olympics, the battles faced and overcome by our Paralympians seem to shine through every sport daily. So many have had to overcome incredibly debilitating conditions to be alive, let alone perform well.

That took my mind back to a Paralympian for whom I had incredible respect. Her name is Janine Shepherd, and she told her story in the book and the movie "Never Tell Me Never". Janine was all set for the Olympic squad when her bike was crushed in a horrific accident. The book is about her incredible fight back, using the power of her spirit to overcome her tragedy. Janine agreed to be a famous guest in my book, "Who'd Be a Parent?" Her story was so inspirational that it couldn't be overlooked in a book on Humble Heroes.

> Obviously, in my adult life, the most difficult time was my accident. The accident happened when I was out training on a pushbike for the '88 Winter Olympics, and it left me – well, they didn't think I would survive, they didn't think I'd walk. I broke my neck and back in four places, my right arm, five ribs on my left side, my collarbone, some bones in my feet, severe lacerations on my body, head injuries, internal injuries, I lost five litres of blood, so I was not in a very good state. Suddenly everything that I had ever, ever valued and worked for was gone in an instant. That was terribly difficult to deal with, and the loss of self-esteem. I hated my body. I couldn't walk – everything I had worked hard for was gone.

> But one of the most important things I have probably learnt from my accident is that I feel everything is there to teach us something. I can look philosophically at things now and think – "Well, what can I learn from this? What's life trying to teach me now?" As it turns out, usually things work out – and sometimes you don't end up going the way you wanted, but you end up on a different tangent, and it is usually a better one. Even when things don't work out the way I want them to or things are a bit tough, I can now step back and go, "Well, I've made it through the toughest battle. I'll make it through this one." As the old saying goes, tough times never last, but tough people do.

> We all need to be optimistic. Life is all about the difference between an optimist and a pessimist. There is only one good thing about a pessimist: they are great to borrow money from because they never expect to get it back.

I also think that parents today provide for their children materially, but I don't think they provide for them emotionally and spiritually. I think the best thing is just to be there. I think we are so busy paying off the house and paying off the mortgage. Both parents are working, but we've got to be there, and we have to work out what our priorities are. I just think that people need to remember their emotional and spiritual development is just as important as providing for them materially.

My recovery has taken a long time. I can now look back and say, "Well, now I can see a reason for it all happening but back then, I couldn't."
I guess the important thing to realise when you are in the middle of tough times — other people have done it, other people have survived, and you will survive. That's got to give you hope — that you are not alone.

Janine, for your inspirational leadership to us all, I enthusiastically welcome you to our Humble Heroes' Hall of Fame.

Editorial comment:
Like Dr John, I am a great admirer of Janine Shepherd. She was once a guest speaker at my school's Speech Night. As always, she was inspirational.

"My message is, you know, life is tough, ... life is hard. But that ... if you can accept that, then it's not hard anymore, ... that it's sort of lean into the hills, lean into the struggles, they're there to teach us something... I think I hold up a mirror, whether I'm on stage or in my books, and people see some part of their life reflected in that."
– Janine Shepherd

Series 7

61. Angela – my good friend Angela gets a lesson from her partner in "Butt-ing out"

62. David – "Doughboy" David learns how to handle bullying using his Feeling Gate

63. Ivan – a lovely story from the Olympics on Ivan conceding victory in the marathon to a more worthy champion

64. Marie – sometimes evidence has to be somewhat personal and Marie and I learn to apply Dr Hunter's formula when you're not sure

65. Elmo – in a class of his own – a wonderful story about love and laughter from a friend with dementia

66. Celebrity contribution: Steve Biddulph – prolific author and advocate for children, gives his assessment on the importance of dads in kids' lives

67. Sandy – motivated by Steve Biddulph's story about dads, Sandy gives us a great lesson in coping as a single mum

68. Renee – Renee's dad would have nothing to do with his infant daughter after the separation but later on Renee was determined to change things

69. Andrew – Andrew Kwong, author of "One Bright Moon", shares an incredible story about resilience, passion, self-belief, sacrificial love, endurance and determination

70. Celebrity contribution: Greg – Yellow Wiggle, Greg Page, talks about how he struggled with the balancing act of career and kids

Story 61

Angela

My good friend Angela gets a lesson
from her partner in "Butt-ing out"

*T*oday's story is about butting out, and I'm sure you have someone in your life that makes this story frustratingly real for you.

Angela is a wonderful lady who believed in me and my vision for the WorryWoos Emotional Intelligence Program for Kids. She took on the program as the Australian distributor.

This year has not been an easy one for Angela. Her mum, Faye is 90 and fiercely independent. She raised three kids in a rural community, having one gorgeous girl with special needs and was widowed at age 32. Faye is made of that true blue Aussie spirit that says, "When the going gets tough, the tough get going."

But, the time has come for a change. Still fiercely independent of mind, Faye has been diagnosed recently with a serious medical condition, which means lots of tests, specialist visits and lots of struggles to do it all with flagging energy. Against her will, Faye has come up to stay with Angela and her husband, Gordon, to make sure Faye can get the treatment she needs.

But, you don't surrender your house, independence, routines, hobbies and friends easily. It is fair to say that independent Faye has been a touch testy. She doesn't want people to fuss and wants to be left alone. She wants to make her own decisions.

In the other corner is her daughter, Angela, who is equally strong-willed, fiercely independent and wants her mum to get the best attention. So here we have two independent ladies, each sure they're doing what's right. According to Gordon, this is how the conversations between them go:

> Angela: "Mum, you have a big day of tests coming up tomorrow. I think you should get some rest."
>
> Faye: "But I don't need to rest now. I'll rest when I need to."
>
> Angela: "But last time we went to the urologist, you were absolutely exhausted the next day."
>
> Faye: "But that was because you had me all uptight about it all."
>
> Angela: "But, mum, it wasn't what I said. Just the walking and the effort and the concentration knocked you around."

Faye:"But it wouldn't have if you stopped fussing."

Angela:"But mum, I have to. It's not that I want to."

Gordon is on the sidelines listening to this loopy conversation and, when asked by Angela to step in and be a bit more supportive, he suggests that both of them should probably just "But" out. In other words, hear each other and take on board what the other is saying, but no more "buts"!

It's easier said than done when you're sure you're right and think the other person isn't listening. But, honestly, have you ever won an argument at all, ever, let alone with the confronting "but" thrown at you like a sparring jab?

What do they say? We have two ears and one tongue, so we should be listening twice as much as we talk. It's hard work, and maybe the other person does have it wrong, but no "but" is going to fix it – leave it alone, walk away, go quiet or even put your point into a text message surrounded by loving packaging – that way, things can be considered rationally without the amygdala jumping in and blocking the ears.

So I pledge that BUT is out, and I BUTT out when I disagree. But if only people would listen to me the first time!!

Editorial comment:
Sound advice, Dr John. Most of us have different views to others on various topics. If only everyone agreed to disagree, the world might be better.

The phrase "to agree to disagree" was first used by John Wesley in 1770 at the death of George Whitefield.

"There are many doctrines of a less essential nature ... In these we may think and let think; we may 'agree to disagree'. But, meantime, let us hold fast the essentials."
– John Wesley

Story 62

David

"Doughboy" David learns how to
handle bullying using his Feeling Gate

*D*avid is my Humble Hero for this story. David was a bright but pale seven-year-old boy who was being teased relentlessly by the older boys in the school.

David's father was the local baker, so because of his pallor and his dad's job, they nicknamed him "doughboy". David hated it so much that he ran away from school and tried to self-harm. When he came into the clinic, I let him hang on to Twitch, the frustrated WorryWoo.

We read the story of Twitch and all the things that frustrated him and made him angry. I used the worry bug and renamed it the put-down bug. The put-down bug kept telling him he was useless, a loser, had no friends, and all the other hurtful words.

I explained what was happening to him. In his brain, he has a "Feeling Gate". Every message he hears has to pass through this feeling gate on its way to the brain. If the message is hurtful, the feeling gate (aka the amygdala) will take over, the brain will cut out, and he will be at the mercy of his anger.

So we decided we would get clever and keep his mind on the job, not let feelings reign. I used the analogy of the submarine hatch; when he came under fire, he would close down the feeling gate, like the hatch on the submarine, and let all the hurtful words go to the counting part of the brain as it had no feelings.

To make sure he kept his mind (not his feelings) on the job, he had to go near the teasers, and say "hi" to them, so they noticed him, and he would count the number of put-downs they tried.

To make sure he could cope, we practised it all in the clinic – with me calling him all the horrible names he had mentioned. If David cried or laughed, that meant he was feeling the words, not counting them so then we would try again. We would keep doing this exercise until he focused on the score, not the sore.

Then armed with his newly found mind-muscle, David was set for the next day. If the stirrers tried to put him down, he could say, "Thank you" or "Have you got any new ones?" but he was to count the words, not feel them.

At the end of each day, when he got home, he had to write his score for the day on the kitchen calendar. I promised him that if he kept his mind on the score rather than feeling the hurt, his score would drop to near zero within two weeks.

David now had mind muscle and mental power. He wasn't at the mercy of the put-down bug anymore!

Kids need gimmicks or concrete strategies; adult words and abstract feelings don't work at that age.

It proved a total success. David outsmarted them, so they left him alone. One of them became his older buddy.

It just reminded me of the power of the mind – if kids can be mentally armed, they're ready for the slings and arrows of outrageous fortune.

I lost a Twitch in the process of this exercise because David had grown attached to it, but what we won would hopefully last him a lifetime.

Editorial comment:
Well done, Dr John. Kids need all the help we can provide to help them through difficult times. As many have done before, Dr John drops in a Shakespeare quotation: an extract from "Hamlet", and one of the most famous speeches in the English language. It is a robust analysis of the morality of suicide in an unbearably painful world.

"To be, or not to be: that is the question:
Whether 'tis nobler in the mind to suffer
The slings and arrows of outrageous fortune
Or to take arms against a sea of troubles,
And by opposing end them?—To die,—to sleep,—
No more; and by a sleep to say we end
The heartache, and the thousand natural shocks."
– "Hamlet" (Act III, Scene i)

Story 63

Ivan

A lovely story from the Olympics on Ivan conceding victory in the marathon to a more worthy champion

In this age of selfish self-promotion, I would forgive you for thinking that those wonderful values of camaraderie and looking after each other have gone forever post-Covid. Certainly, I've seen people turning on each other, avoiding each other, selfishly emptying the shelves of toilet paper and then selling it on the black market. We'd be forgiven for saying the pandemic has brought out the best and worst in human behaviour.

So it was incredibly uplifting when I received this note from Mick, a Humble Heroes listener, about an event in the marathon in the Tokyo Olympics right in the middle of the pandemic.

He writes,

> "I'm just forwarding this extract from CNN news yesterday. It gave me an incredible lift, and I thought it might do the same for others."

> Kenyan runner Abel Mutai was just a few metres from the finish line but got confused by the signage and stopped, thinking he had finished the race. A Spanish runner, Ivan Fernandez, running behind him, realised what was happening and started yelling at the Kenyan, "Keep running! Keep running!" Abel Mutai did not know Spanish and did not understand it, so the Spaniard assisted Abel right in the middle of that gruelling race and pointed him in the right direction. Abel Mutai could go on and claim the victory, beating the Spaniard.

> A journalist asked Ivan why he did that, and Ivan replied,

> "I dream that one day we can have a kind of community life in which we push each other and help each other to win."

> The journalist pressed, "But why did you let the Kenyan win?"

> Ivan replied, "I didn't let him win. He was already going to win. The race was his."

> The journalist insisted, "But you could have won!"

> Ivan looked at him and replied, "But what would be the merit of my victory? What would be the honour of that medal? What would my mother think of that?"

We pass down our values from generation to generation. So what values are we teaching our children? Let's not teach our children the ruthless road to winning. Instead, let's pass on the beauty and humanity of offering a helping hand.

Chivalry, sacrifice, integrity, love, honesty, kindness and friendship are all still there, below the surface, often too scared to come out because they don't feel safe.

Let's do what we can to help them flourish. Well done, Ivan, you may not have won that gold medal, but you score big gold in my Humble Heroes' Hall of Fame.

Editorial comment:
In that race, the Spanish runner knew that if he won, it would have been an empty win — a Pyrrhic victory. Every war has its casualties, every success has its price and sometimes it's not worth paying.

The phrase "Pyrrhic victory" is named after King Pyrrhus of Epirus, whose armies defeated the more powerful Roman armies at Heraclea in 280 BC and Asculum in 279 BC. In both victories, the victors had more casualties than the losers.
"Another such victory, and I'll return to Epirus alone."
— King Pyrrhus

Story 64

Marie

Sometimes evidence has to be somewhat personal
and Marie and I learn to apply Dr Hunter's
formula when you're not sure

One of the significant influences on my attitude to life was my friend Hunter, a brilliant surgeon and neighbour. Outside his brilliance in the operating theatre was another soul searching, like me, for humour to relieve the stress and strains of our demanding jobs.

One of the things Hunter taught me was, in the absence of evidence, to use your own homegrown experience as fact.

Hunter used it, for instance, when patients would ask him about the standard frequency of having sex with one's partner. He would check on the patient's average, then mentally compare it with his performance, and, nearly every time, would inform the anxious patient with the good news that they were above average, and everyone was happy.

I needed his startling statistical research evidence with Marie. Marie was in a bad way. She told me she was "as hoarse as a hyena with throat nodules."

After a cup of tea, she told me she had used up all her throat leather trying to referee her kids' fights. "Tell me, Doc, is their fighting average, above average or am I just one of the lucky ones and don't realise it?" she croaked.

I decided to try out a checklist:

"Do you or your husband have any favourites because that can cause fights?"

"No favourites, Doc, they're both pains."

"Do you and your husband fight a lot, and the kids are just copying?" I asked, hoping for the big breakthrough.

"About average, I'd say," she groaned.

"Have you been feeling depressed lately? That can cause attention-seeking fights."

"No more than usual. About average," was her casual reply.

"Do you have a general problem managing the kids?" I urged.

"Oh no. We have to yell to get them to do anything but so does everybody."

"Does your husband help, or are the kids fighting to catch his attention?" I was now desperate for a lead.

"Like most men, he can't see the problem because he's not around enough to know. But that's normal," she sighed.

"Last question. Do you think you should go and get professional help?"

Marie just looked at me. "That's why I'm here, Doctor John!"

Of course, she was! I was embarrassed, but I smiled reassuringly and said that 99 per cent of kids fight. "But, Doctor John, is six times a day worse than average or what?"

Faced with this demand for an absolute answer, I used the Hunter home-spun method. I counted my domestic tally with my kids and then pronounced Marie average.

She sat back, I sat back, she grinned, and I grinned. Now Marie was ready to hear and work on an action plan to improve those family dynamics.

But at that moment, Marie had found peace in the knowledge that she was not bad and not alone.

As Alvin Toffler said, "Parenting is the last province of the amateur." Talented as we all might be in many areas, Marie and I agreed that we were both beautifully average that day.

Editorial comment:
For some people, "good" is never good enough – you either know one of these people or you are one. It's good to hear Dr John extolling the beauty of being average. "To want to be better is human, but perfectionism may be detrimental to our mental health", according to psychologist and author Honor Jane Newman.

"Perfectionism is so common but is not discussed out in the open the way other conditions are. It is important for perfectionists to realize they don't have to stay stuck and unhappy."
– Honor Jane Newman

Story 65

Elmo

In a class of his own – a wonderful story about
love and laughter from a friend with dementia

$\mathcal{I}$ hope you have someone in your life as precious as Elmo. He was brought up during the Depression, got a scholarship to Teachers' College, taught in the Outback for years, and became a School Principal. He was one of those Principals who knew every kid and spent his time in the classroom helping kids struggling with reading.

In addition, Elmo was the most incredible grower of home veggies. He also brewed his beer, made the best apple jelly ever and, each month, provided a boot full of homegrown plants to boost the coffers of the Lions' Club.

Elmo was a wise man. He said, when you retire, don't move away from your forwards. Stay where you know, with people you know and where you have the services you want. That's what I did.

Elmo also had a tremendous sense of humour. No matter his pain or problem, he would find a way to laugh. Elmo taught me a lot about the power of laughter, and I started to analyse the role of laughter in our lives.

A few years ago, Arthur Stone, Professor of Psycho-neurology at the University of New York, identified a group of life-enhancing chemicals, including the antibody Immunoglobin A, that are triggered when we laugh.

This antibody in the mucus, which lines the nose, helps fight all sorts of illnesses and diseases by identifying bacteria, viruses and even potential tumour cells. According to Dr Peter Spitzer, founder of Australia's Humour Foundation, laughing for just 10 minutes will achieve the following:

- drive carbon dioxide out of the body and replace it with oxygen

- produce anti-inflammatory agents that fight back pain and arthritis

- encourage the muscles to relax

- reduce levels of serum cortisol, the stress hormone

- boost the immune system responses

- boost the production of feel-good endorphins

We're programmed to laugh away our woes. If you don't believe me, think of the worst problem you're facing, then turn the corners of your mouth into a grin and then feel the difference.

But back to Elmo, and I assure you he wouldn't have minded the diversion. Anyhow, he had one significant weakness, his age. Unfortunately, with age came dementia. His golf mates and I would visit him in the dementia ward regularly, and even though eventually he forgot how to dress and even who we were, he was so loved by doctors and staff because he could always laugh.

Finally, it took its terminal toll and the last time I visited him before he died, he could not talk intelligibly and couldn't even hold his cup to drink his juice, nor did he know who I was.

But as I handed him his cup, he held it aloft, a grin came on his face, and he mumbled, "Ladies and Gentlemen" as if he was about to propose a toast.

Elmo, you are my Humble Hero, and I raise my glass to you!

Editorial comment:
As I've said before, laughter is the best medicine. I'm showing my age by quoting from Bob Newhart, one of my favourite comics from the twentieth century. He became famous in the 1960s for his deadpan comedy routines.

"Laughter gives us distance. It allows us to step back from an event, deal with it and then move on."
– Bob Newhart

Story 66

Steve

Steve Biddulph, prolific author and advocate
for children, gives his assessment on the
importance of dads in kids' lives

Celebrity Contribution

$\mathcal{I}$'m a great fan of Steve Biddulph, the famous author of "Raising Boys", "Manhood", "Secrets of Happy Children" and other works. We often lectured together, and some years ago, I received a personal email from him concerning his research on the role of dads in kids' lives. He says,

Children with fathers living at home:

Get better results at school and are more likely to go to university

Are less likely to get into trouble at school

Are better at mathematics and reading

Have higher levels of compassion and empathy, and self-esteem

Are less likely to be violent or victims of violence

Are less likely to be victims of sexual abuse or assault

Are less likely to get in trouble with the law

Are less likely to commit suicide or get involved with drugs

Are less likely to get pregnant, or get someone pregnant, during their teens

They are more likely to have happy marriages and be good parents themselves.

Now that can't always happen, but to any dads out there, separated or not, re-partnered or not, angry or not, be aware that your role in kids' lives is so pervasive; the more involved a father can be with his children, the more these benefits grow. Even a divorced or separated father can keep the positive benefits if he stays involved. Kids need dads. It's as simple as that.

And it's not just for the benefit of the kids either. Did you read those University of NSW statistics a while back? Executives are severely damaging their health and family life with the demands of the job. Longer and longer hours, with more and more unpaid overtime. And what is the goal? To climb the corporate ladder or spawn bigger business for more and more money to achieve more and more? What?

The University of NSW statistics remind me of the story of the holidaying Sydney executive up on the coast after the lockdown lift. He was strolling along Patonga Beach and caught up with a laid-back local fisherman. This man told the executive that he fished enough on his trawler to keep the family happily fed and, with the rest of his time, he just read, played with the kids, sat out on his verandah with his partner and soaked up the sun.

"Look", said the executive, "I know there's money in this game. If you worked longer, you'd soon be able to buy a fleet of boats, have people work for you, move to the city and start exporting. And after 20 years of hard work, you could retire here for life!"

"And then do what?" said the fisherman. "My kids will have grown up and gone, probably wouldn't want to know me, and all I'd have is a big empty house to show off to who?"

Funny, even to this day, we think of mothering as a lifetime job but still think of fathering as a 10-second job. To all the dads and mums out there doing their best, today you're my Humble Heroes.

Editorial comment:
I'm also a Steve Biddulph fan although unlike Dr John, I am not able to call him a friend. I was however influenced by his work and that of the Boys in Schools Program centred at the University of Newcastle in the 1980s. These days we have come around to be more questioning of the traditional roles of parents in the nuclear family and its many variants. This piece reflects attitudes and assumptions that may no longer be valid in some people's minds. Nevertheless the story is interesting and thought provoking.

"I have become more comfortable and challenged by the role of being a dad. My life is so much happier. I do not spend time with my children out of a sense of guilt or obligation, but because it feeds my soul and is a job I am proud of doing well. I often feel painfully unprepared and frequently 'get it wrong'."
– Steve Biddulph, "Manhood"

Sandy

Motivated by Steve Biddulph's story about
dads, Sandy gives us a great lesson in coping
as a single mum

Podcast Listener's Humble Hero

I recently had a letter from a lady called Sandy, which said in part:

I heard your podcast the other day in praise of dads, separated or not. Well, I lived with an unbelievably deceitful guy. We separated years ago, but what a nightmare. I learnt a lot and wanted to share it with other women going through tough times.

The worst feeling is that you're just a pawn in a court game. You're just somebody who has no rights in the custody situation, and the other person is suddenly calling all the shots. It's the power that they have over you that left me feeling so angry and helpless.

My advice to other mothers going through this sort of hell is to be gentle with yourself and separate your feelings from the kids'. The way I coped was to draw an imaginary bubble around myself and the kids, and then try to deal with their feelings separate from mine.

I guess what I'm saying then is to listen to their complaints and be their wailing wall, not their military adviser! If they come back from access weekends with complaints or fears and tears, don't feel that you've got to get the liquid paper out and repair their weekend. Sometimes they really want just someone who will sit there and listen to them and comfort them, but not take some counter-action.

Apply a little bit of light-heartedness to the situation too. How often do they complain about not wanting to go to school, not wanting to go to bed or not being able to watch a video? For some reason, we tend to put access on an entirely different line than anything else. Be sort of realistic about what they're complaining about.

I've learnt over time to permit them and encourage them to love their dad regardless of how he has treated you.

But there's another side to custody that books seem to overlook. That is, it's not just you, and it's not just the kids. There are relatives, parents, and friends who aren't used to access. They will come up with the classic line, "Well, I just wouldn't put up with it. I wouldn't send my children." This makes you feel like you're a complete ratbag. Thank God for a couple of sensible friends who helped me keep my balance.

Because the simple fact is that, legally, you don't have that choice.

Legally the children have a right to see their dad and their dad has a right to see the kids.

So don't fight about it, and don't fuel your anger with their comments. Let them say what they want to say, but don't make it ammunition for your little war."

—Sandy

Thanks Sandy — it's so true. It's hard for the kids to stay afloat if you've sunk the other end of the boat.

> **Editorial comment:**
> The HelpGuide International Website explains that successful co-parenting means that your own emotions — any anger, resentment, or hurt — must take a back seat to the needs of your children. Admittedly, setting aside such strong feelings may be the hardest part of learning to work cooperatively with your ex, but it's also perhaps the most vital.

Story 68

Renee

Renee's dad would have nothing to do with his infant daughter after the separation. Later on Renee was determined to change things

Renee was the only daughter of a single mum with a chronic back condition that kept her bedridden for much of the time. Darryl, her dad, was nowhere to be seen and as Renee grew up she became very bitter about a dad who would have nothing to do with her.

When she came to my attention, she was self-harming and cutting on her wrists and forearms and refusing to go to school. She just wanted nothing to do with a rejecting world. Renee then went through a gothic phase, withdrew into her room, and was often found curled up embryonically.

Her paternal grandfather agreed to pay for Renee to attend an "alternate" school focused on the performing arts. Every student there would probably have been rated as an alternate. No school uniforms, of course, and the students did online distance education for the first half of the day before various facets of performing arts in the afternoon.

Renee took to the acting side of the afternoon activities and soon earned leading roles. She was super bright, and it took her no time to learn her part. Eventually, we prevailed on Darryl, her dad, to help out a bit with private singing lessons so Renee could also be confident in Musicals.

But Renee couldn't accept that her dad wouldn't even think about supporting her or wanting anything to do with her. As Renee progressed into more challenging roles, she did a lot of role play – putting herself in the position of various characters. What motivated them? Why were they bitter? Why were they angry?

After we won a bit more money from dad, Renee started to put her feet in dad's shoes, this man she had never met. He was only 17 years old when she was conceived, given no say in her schooling or location, and embarrassed and ridiculed by his friends. He was a chip off the old block and didn't know how to show affection. He was just like his own dad.

Darryl saw his dad's payment of Renee's school fees as a pathetic attempt to make up for lost love, and that's why he would have no part of it.

Renee put herself in Darryl's shoes, and together we composed an email to Darryl:

> *Dad, I now understand how hard it must have been when I was born, and I'm sure no one has ever really understood why you have never been*

part of my life. That's not your fault, and it's not mine, but I need to feel you care about me, and I would like to buy you a ticket to the matinee session of the play we're putting on. You will be my only guest for that performance.

Dad went, they talked, they now catch up regularly, and the family is more or less functional.

Although I was there to help Renee, she taught me how much repair work can be done in relationships if we temporarily drop all our anger, hurt and rejection and try to walk in the other person's shoes. Very few people I've met, and I've met some tough ones, are deliberately nasty. Most are wearing unaddressed pain that makes them spit their way through life.

Darryl's problem was not Renee. Once he shifted his focus, he was free to love again. Thank you, Renee. What you did took real courage! I'm so proud to have known you.

Editorial comment:
Dr John talks about walking in the other person's shoes. There is a poem on this topic (as well as a song by Elvis) by Mary Torrans Lathrap (1838-1895). It was initially titled "Judge Softly" in 1895 and has later become known as Walk a Mile in His Moccasins.

Here is an extract:
"Brother, there, but for the grace of God go you and I.
Just for a moment, slip into his mind and traditions
And see the world through his spirit and eyes
Before you cast a stone or falsely judge his conditions.
Remember to walk a mile in his moccasins
And remember the lessons of humanity taught to you by your elders.
We will be known forever by the tracks we leave behind
In other people's lives, our kindnesses and generosity. Take the time to walk a mile in his moccasins."
– Mary T. Lathrap, 1895

Story 69

Andrew

Andrew Kwong, author of "One Bright Moon,"
shares an incredible story about resilience,
passion, self-belief, sacrificial love,
endurance and determination

*M*aybe you can be inspired by Andrew, just as I have been. And if you think you've got it tough, reading Andrew's autobiography has made me feel like I've been on sweet street! They say you can see the stars only when things are dark. Well, his book, "One Bright Moon", bears testimony to that one-liner. It's a remarkable book and has won national awards.

When Andrew and I got together recently over a cup of coffee, I realised our books were both partially motivated by a common goal – we wanted to convey to our kids and grandkids that life can be challenging and for them to develop an attitude of gratitude rather than entitlement.

The back cover of Andrew's book says it all. "Andrew Kwong was only seven when he witnessed his first execution – months later, it was his own father on trial. This time the sentence was banishment to a re-education camp, not death. It left the family tainted, despised and with few means of survival during the terrible years of persecution and famine known as the Great Leap Forward. Escape seemed the only solution."

So severe was the famine, in China, that one bowl of rice had to be triple-cooked to bulk out their sense of survival. Because their grandfather historically had more money than the masses, they were expected to house and feed others and treated as traitors for any enterprise they showed. His family tried to migrate, but the regime needed their money sent from relatives outside China. Escape was their only hope. That meant enormous risk and when Andrew was smuggled alone out of China he had to hide in the bow of the boat which ferried them across to avoid detection, repatriation and more punishment.

But Andrew's dedication to his family and his determination to fulfil their wishes for him to get a good education made him go to incredible lengths to achieve. His family told him La Salle College in Kowloon was the best school for him, but they had no vacancies.

Day after day, Andrew would walk to the College, sit outside this prestigious school's Headmaster's office, and read "Hamlet" while hoping for an interview. His persistence finally paid off. Five weeks later, the Headmaster's door swung open and he was accepted.

However, back on the mainland, things were deteriorating. Persecutions were increasing, war threats were becoming more ominous, and Andrew wanted to get as far away as possible – and Australia was as far as he could imagine. With his parents' blessing and several hair-raising close calls, Andrew finally made it to Australia and enrolled at Holy Cross College in Ryde.

Andrew became the resident barber/hairdresser to pay his way through school. Through hard work and dedication Andrew did well enough at school to make it into Medicine. To make his way through Medicine at the University of NSW, Andrew became a Chinese restaurant waiter. With the same persistence and resilience Andrew got through Medicine.

Then he met and married Sheree and moved into private practice on the Central Coast. This is where I met him as the Consultant Psychologist at Central Coast Grammar School, where his children were enrolled.

Things were good professionally and personally, but his family was still split. Fortunately, post Mao, with relationships warming between East and West his mother, Wai-Syn, was allowed to migrate. That finally happened in June 1989, and just reading Andrew's recounting of the joys of that reunion certainly brought me to tears.

Andrew finishes his story with words from his dad at that reunion, but the message is to us all. "Ordinary people like us, throughout history, are often made to suffer by forces beyond their control. The sea may be vast and treacherous, but we must steer our boats. Hold on to hope and your life with both hands, always and forever."

Andrew, welcome to my Humble Heroes' Hall of Fame.

Editorial comment:
Andrew Kwong is an extraordinary man with a stoical outlook on life. Thank you, Dr John, for bringing his wisdom and fortitude to our attention. I'm sure many readers like me will want to read "One Bright Moon".

"Accept the things to which fate binds you, and love the people with whom fate brings you together, but do so with all your heart."
— Marcus Aurelius

Story 70

Greg

Yellow Wiggle Greg talks about how
he struggled with the balancing act of
career and kids

Celebrity Contribution

*I*f you were born after 1970, or even before, you would share my delight in meeting a very Humble Hero, the very famous and oh-so-humble yellow Wiggle, Greg Page, who was a student of mine when the Wiggles were doing Early Childhood teacher training in Sydney. Now, if ever there was a busy superstar Greg was it!

I asked Greg when he was at the height of his busy career to pen a few thoughts on parenting. Here is part of his reply.

> *Being a Wiggle means being away from home and, in turn, being away from my family. This puts a great deal of stress on the relationships within my family at various times. Even when I am at home, we still may be performing during the day, having meetings, recording, filming or just looking after general business issues.*
>
> *This does not leave much time for me to spend with Michelle. When I do happen to have a day off with no meetings or photo shoots, then Michelle usually marks it in my diary for me as a day for us to spend together.*
>
> *Of course, like many parents, we face the same issues in dealing with children's behaviour. For me, this is where the Early Childhood teaching course was invaluable. One thing that we learnt was that you always set boundaries and never let the boundaries be broken. In other words, in our house, if a rule is made, it is made for a reason and should not be broken.*
>
> *And, of course, with punishment comes the obligatory, "You all hate me." Well yes, we get that too. Again, teacher training has helped me here. We were always taught never to say anything negative about the* **person** *if there is a problem but to focus on the behaviour. It is usually the behaviour that they are exhibiting which is the problem.*
>
> *Sometimes when I am the person handing out the punishment, I am met with comments like, "I wish you were away on tour" or "Mum would let me do it." This is hard to deal with because there is a part of you that believes you are not wanted and a part that sees it just as a way of getting to you.*

Whatever the reason, you just have to deal with it the best way possible. Usually, I just keep very calm, don't let the anger show, and say something like, "Well, I'm not on tour, so you'll just have to do it" or "I'm not mum, and either way, a rule is a rule." It might not be a very clever answer to the problem, but it is a controlled response with no inappropriate or violent reaction.

Greg, you're just human and a very authentic one at that! What an incredible contribution you have made to the lives of so many for so long. It is with great humility and respect that I welcome you to the Humble Heroes' Hall of Fame.

Editorial comment:
As a grandparent, I am accustomed to watching the Wiggles and remember the original yellow Wiggle before the group made changes to the line-up. I like Greg's pragmatic approach to being a parent. Solutions to problems don't always have to be clever – just as long as they work! Keep it simple.

Occam's Razor principle is often attributed to William of Occam in the C14th, even though he didn't invent the rule. Others had favoured the "keep it simple" concept Occam embraced, but no one as relentlessly as he did, causing 19th-century Scottish philosopher Sir William Hamilton to forever link Occam with the idea of cutting away redundant material.

Series 8

71. Jerome – Jerome provides an incredible example of walking the talk on sustainability

72. Kerry – Kerry shows us the impact good teachers can make on children's well being

73. Podcast listener's humble hero: Bert – an inspirational story from a reader about his dad, and the "bell of hope" custom in cancer treatment

74. Podcast listener's humble hero: Julie – Julie has paid a high price for her liver transplant but what an incredible contribution she has made to her family and the sporting community

75. Patrick – this remarkable but very humble man, at the peak of his conducting career, has a major accident with a circular saw that threatens his career

76. Tahlia – when kids' bad imagination has them petrified, logic won't work but powerful good imagination can often do the trick

77. Podcast listener's humble hero: Duncan – Duncan's dad was neither humble nor, (in the eyes of his family) heroic, but the ashes test sorted it out and peace was restored

78. Timmy – our Timmy's life may have been short but his legacy lives on in our family

79. Author vs Editor – a light-hearted lesson for the editor that good outcomes often take devious routes

80. Judy – assistant editor Judy writes an inspirational piece about her father that shifts the author's attitude to his own dad

Jerome

Jerome provides an incredible example of
walking the talk on sustainability

We hear many prominent citizens posturing about climate change and sustainability yet living the good life with all the frills. It's hard to have any respect for them or their message. Then I met up with Jerome, and all my prejudice got blown out of the water. I do hope you have someone in your life like Jerome.

Part of Jerome's message is about water. Jerome, his partner, and his daughter Mara live on a small farm in our community. They catch and recirculate their water, nothing spectacular about that. But Jerome has commenced an aquaponics project that represents the best of the best. I'm not the only one who thinks that way. Last year he was selected to present his scheme at an International Sustainability Conference in Paris.

It involves using herbivore fish (silver perch) in the top tank. Solar power circulates the nutrient run-off from that tank to plants being grown hydroponically, and the run-off from the plants is fed back to the fish tank, so the cycle is self-regulating.

But that's only one project. Jerome and his family also collect throw-away fruit and vegetables from local fruit shops, which they crush for the gardens. Their chooks enjoy the composted vegetables, and the crushed-up oyster shells they eat make stronger eggshells. Jerome even recirculates toilet waste, has beehives, and has planted melaleucas so the honey can have the same medicinal properties as Manuka honey.

The family ride push bikes to work and school, keep their electricity usage to a minimum and live a life in as much accord with nature as suburban life can offer. On invitation, Jerome has initiated sustainable practices in several local schools where he assists teachers in setting up class gardens and beehives and separating waste. He also helps them to grow their vegetables, and to green up the canteen.

At every opportunity Jerome is up on my roof, cleaning out my gutters and repairing holes in the roof. He helps re-paint my driveway and checks my worm farm, which he donated. He's a good guy, and the only time I've seen him get cross was when I threw out my used coffee ground cakes into the rubbish bin! I have since repented, of course. Despite all this, Jerome is a clear-thinking and intelligent good guy. He's that "normal"; he will even share a glass of red with me!

Jerome is too good to be true. When I confronted him with the challenge of what motivates him to live such a good and generous and neighbourly life, I was confident he would have a solid religious answer. Jerome shook his head. His motive was just to enjoy doing his bit for the planet and helping others in any way possible.

Maybe you have someone in your circle of friends like Jerome; if so, nurture them. If not, perhaps, like me, you can start your journey and, in time, aspire to be as good as my Saint Jerome.

You may remember the story I did on 12-year-old Jonathan Wilson-Fuller, the boy who was allergic to the environment. I recall him commenting that our contributions to save the planet might just constitute a drop in the ocean, but those drops collectively made the ocean.

Jerome, I'm hoping to continue to improve my footprint on this delicate planet and maybe just by retelling your story, others can pick up the baton and follow your lead long after I've let go.

Editorial comment:
Jerome could be described as a climate activist, but he might not like the term. He inspired Dr John with his practical efforts to help save the planet – a great example of thinking globally and acting locally. An inspiration not only to Dr John, but hopefully to many of us – including our politicians.

"Our politicians do not need to wait for anyone else in order to start taking action. Nor do they need conferences, treaties, international agreements or outside pressure. They could start right away."
– Greta Thunberg

Story 72

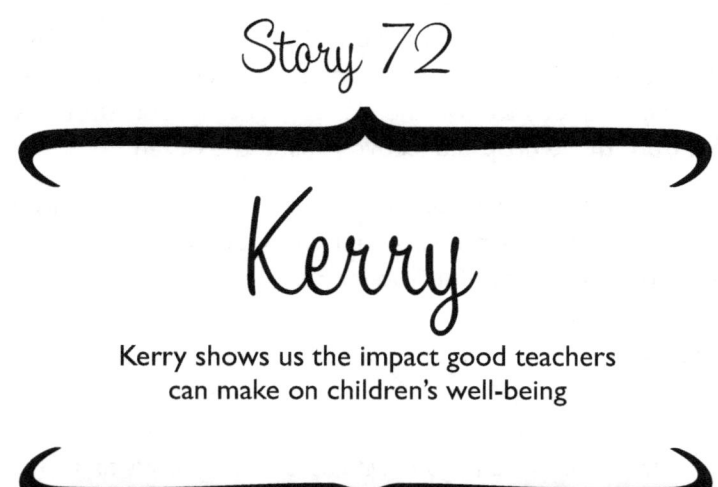

Kerry

Kerry shows us the impact good teachers
can make on children's well-being

*L*et me share Kerry's story. It has nothing to do with the pandemic but everything to do with the remarkable role of the teacher. As we tentatively came out of our shelters and bunkers after the pandemic and the children came out of homeschooling and back to the classroom, many parents suddenly realised what an incredible job teachers do.

Many years ago I was supervising students at a school in the inner city. There were two kids in Kindy who immediately drew my attention. Their real names were Michael and Mark, but the teacher's aide called them M and M – she claimed you had to bribe them with M&M's to get them to do anything!

They both took so long to move, work, finish anything, and answer. But like every label we load on kids, there are the back stories we need to tell.

Michael had always been slow to walk, talk, learn his colours, and learn nursery rhymes; anything and everything took time. His parents had taken him to paediatricians and psychologists, but their message was clear. They could do nothing to speed Michael up. He was a slow learner.

Mark had always been normal for all his milestones. But his parents were involved in a bitter divorce dispute. He was shunted from one parent to the other, each blaming the other, of course, and when neither of them could fit Mark into their schedule, he would go off to Grandma, whose husband had a terminal medical condition.

Both boys were in a fog: both took forever to do anything, but one was intellectual in origin, and the other was emotional. Mark was so confused and sad that he didn't know who he was. Sometimes he'd even say, "Give that to Mark," when he wanted something.

But, come in, Kerry! This Kindy teacher organised a unique program for Michael, giving him as many accolades as the other kids. When she couldn't get Mark's parents up to see her, she reported that he was "at risk" and eventually met both parents. Then, with the help of the Specialist Counsellor for Emotionally Disturbed Children, she set out to win Mark's confidence, eye contact, cuddles and smile.

And for both M & M's, she was able to hook into the school's "Kookaburra" reward system; each time any of the kids did something good (e. g. finished work, answered a question), they received a "Kookaburra" certificate. Pupils could trade 10 of these neat certificates for a "Golden Kookaburra" award, and then 10 Golden Kookaburras earned the "00" badge!

This badge earned special privileges such as eating lunch inside, sitting on chairs at assembly, a memorable end-of-term excursion, a particular line at the canteen and special borrowing rights at the library.

The last time I heard from them, M & M had both earnt their "00" badge, and their eyes were wide awake.

Thank you to Kerry and all the dedicated teachers doing so much for so many!

Editorial comment:
Teachers like Kerry demonstrate why so many of us think that teaching is the most important job in the world. My wish is that it might also be the most satisfying job in the world.

"Great teachers: are open to learning and improvement; are professionals who are respected for providing structured environments where learning can take place; are knowledgeable and passionate about their subject; inspire more questions and fan the flames of wonder; and are these things and do these things so as to provide students with hope and the opportunity to contribute creatively to the world in need of transformation."
– David de Carvalho, Australian Curriculum Assessment
* and Reporting Authority*

Story 73

Bert

An inspirational story from a reader about
his dad, and the "bell of hope" custom in
cancer treatment

Podcast Listener's Humble Hero

$\mathcal{E}$veryone knows someone who has had cancer. The very word strikes fear into us all, so it's a bit of a novelty when I hear of someone with cancer who strikes a bell!

I recently received a letter from a listener whose Humble Hero is his dad. Ken wrote:

> You know my dad, Bert, and you also know he's my humble hero, annoying and self-opinionated though he may be. Dad and mum split up when I was a young fella but dad was always there for me and my sister, no matter what.

> When I left school, I became dad's apprentice as a chippie and learnt a helluva lot. What struck me most was his incredible work ethic, his integrity, the way he'd honour his word and his handshake even if the client was in the wrong. I was constantly amazed at his ability to make a joke out of work crises and that's not even to mention what an incredible name he had with everyone for being a bloody good builder. It's a fact that most of his long term friends have been his clients, and I'd venture to suggest that that would be rare between builder and client.

> Dad's now retired and I've left the building game but still he lends his tools, freely lends his advice, and never hesitates to give me a hand with my own renovations, nor with his grandad duties taking our four-year-old son to swimming regularly.

> But the reason I'm writing is that this awesome, grumpy old man had emphysema from all the building asbestos, was riddled with rheumatism, both knees had gone, and his bung shoulder prevented him lifting anything above his head. The only thing his specialist found that wasn't buggered was his right instep! Dad hated whingers and if someone was full of moans about their health, dad would ask them about their right instep. That usually threw them off-guard and he could change the subject.

> However, just a few months ago, to add to this load, dad was diagnosed with cancer. Now with all he had going against him, I think most of us would have been happy to curl up our toes and let fate take its toll. But that's not dad. He would ride down to the treatment centre on his old pushie, charm all the secretaries with his loud, upbeat humour and

slightly off-colour jokes and undertake week after week of painful, enervating radiation that left him weak and exhausted.

But last week was different. The specialist pronounced him all clear! Apparently at cancer clinics all around the world, there is a bell that hangs near the door on the way out. No one is allowed to ring that bell until their treatment is all finished or they are pronounced all clear. Last week was dad's turn. He thanked the staff and they gave Bert permission to ring that bell. Dad was grinning from ear to ear and so was every other patient because it meant hope – hope that the treatment will end and that the battle can be won.

I don't know if you've come across this custom before but I just wanted to share the story while I can still hear that bell ringing in our ears. My Humble Hero lives on!

I hadn't heard of the bell-ringing custom in cancer clinics so I checked it out, and Ken's right. It is an increasingly widespread custom. It's thought that the tradition began at the MD Anderson Cancer Center, Texas in 1996.

A Rear Admiral in the U. S. Navy, Irve LeMoyne, was undergoing radiation therapy for head and neck cancer. He told his doctor that he planned to follow the Navy tradition of ringing a bell to signify "when the job was done". He brought a brass bell to his last treatment, rang it several times and left it as a donation. They mounted it on a wall plaque in the main building's Radiation Treatment Centre with the inscription:

Ringing out
Ring this bell
Three times well
Its toll to clearly say,
My treatment's done
This course is run
And I am on my way!

Maybe this story has been more of a clanger than a bell-ringer for you, but if you listen hard enough, and scope wide enough, perhaps someone you love has something to cheer about.

Editorial comment:
There is only one possible way to summarise this powerful story and
that is by quoting from John Donne.

"No man is an island, entire of itself; every man is a piece of the
continent, a part of the main; if a clod be washed away by the sea,
Europe is the less, as well as if a promontory were, as well as if a
manor of thy friend's or of thine own were; any man's death diminishes
me, because I am involved in mankind, and therefore never send to
ask for whom the bell tolls; it tolls for thee."
— John Donne

Julie

Julie has paid a high price for her liver
transplant but what an incredible
contribution she has made to her family
and the sporting community

Podcast Listener's Humble Hero

$\mathcal{I}$'m not talking about your "besties", your special friends who are always there for you. Talking to them brings you regular relief, and we all need those. I'm talking about those other characters, your Humble Heroes, whose lives and lessons have inspired you to be a better person or be grateful for what you've got. Have you noticed that most of these characters have had to overcome adversity? Very few have been born with a silver spoon.

One such character is a very humble person who showed my friend Stan what digging deep is all about. Stan wrote this to me.

I boarded with Julie's parents when, as a 19-year-old, I began my teaching career many years ago at an isolated one-teacher school near the top of the Great Dividing Range in southern NSW.

At the end of that year, Julie was granted special permission to leave school, four and a half months short of her 15th birthday, having derived limited joy from her few years of secondary schooling through correspondence school.

I was fortunate that Julie's parents looked after me in those first challenging years of teaching and became lifelong friends. They may not have been well-educated themselves but I certainly learned from them many useful lessons about living a full and inclusive life.

When she grew up, Julie, an only child, tended to see me as a surrogate brother, so I was dismayed but not surprised when she rang me one day to say that, because of a misadventure not of her own making, her liver was failing and she was going to have a liver transplant, at that time a procedure not without considerable risk. She was rightly fearful, hence her call, but realised there was little alternative.

Fortunately, the long-ago transplant has turned out well for her, and she is now in her mid-70s, helping her own two sons and grandchildren who provide her with much enjoyment.

Julie has remained positive and cheerful, choosing as much as possible to live life to the full, an example being her regular participation in the biennial Australian Transplant Games, where she has consistently won medals for her performances. Her successes in the cricket ball throwing competition seem very apt, given that her father was a keen and skilful cricketer, captain of the local team in which I played alongside him for three years.

Her continuing passion means she is now looking forward to the World Transplant Games. She is a great role model for her young granddaughter who has been selected to play cricket at an interstate level and participate in elite junior training squads.

Another of Julie's achievements has been learning the art of making her own cards for use at birthdays, Christmas times and other celebrations. She is self-taught but has become impressively good at it, so I always look forward to receiving her latest creations, some of which are highly elaborate, often three-dimensional, and all of which are beautiful objects. A few years back, Julie gave me a boxed set of 10 of her cards as a Christmas gift, and it was a challenge to my selflessness that I had to accept that I should use them as intended and give them to others.

Over the past few years, Julie has had to face a new setback, suffering recurring outbreaks of skin cancers as a side effect of the anti-rejection drugs she has taken since her transplant. These skin cancers require her to travel to Sydney to excise them, with painful skin grafts often needed as part of the treatment. Despite no prospect of relief from this latest curse, only an ongoing series of energy-draining visits to specialists every three months, Julie remains positive and determined to keep life as normal as possible.

I hope to keep receiving her creative cards for many years. I certainly admire her resilience and determination, which make her a true humble hero for me.

I wonder whether Julie's cancer clinic has a bell (as in Bert's story) to signal the completion of treatment and the "all-clear"? And whether she will ever get the chance to ring it? I'd imagine she can hear it anyhow.

Story 75

Patrick

This remarkable but very humble man, at the peak
of his conducting career, had a major accident
with a circular saw that threatened his career

How is it that some people, when faced with a setback, become a victim, and others have some weird drive that propels them to kick back?

Compared to many, I've never really faced crippling adversity, so I'm not an expert, but we can admire those who stare such life crushers in the face and do not stay down. It's a gift.

One such person in my life is Patrick! Patrick had everything going for him and was at the peak of his career. He was the Artistic Director of the Central Coast Conservatorium and a talented bassoon player. A brilliant conductor, he was selected to conduct the Tasmanian Symphony Orchestra. He was known and admired throughout NSW schools, but he had one weakness. He was accident-prone. His first accident was letting his voice break when he was Head Chorister of the Sydney Children's Choir. I don't suppose we can blame him for that, but other misfortunes were self-inflicted.

An ordinary bloke, Patrick liked to get out and about, into the surf, into his boat, into the backyard. After his voice broke, he took to the bassoon, but this budding bassoon player tried his luck in the big waves and damaged his neck so that he couldn't carry the bassoon. He turned to conducting, and again he was an outstanding success. Then last year, while cutting old wood with a circular saw in his backyard, the saw jumped on a timber knot and sliced his left hand, virtually severing it.

As they loaded him into the Care Flight helicopter, the expectation was that he was heading for amputation. By chance a specialist micro-surgeon was on duty when Patrick arrived at Royal North Shore Hospital. Ten hours later, Patrick emerged with his hand intact and then the long, laborious process of getting bones, muscles, tendons and ligaments to agree to talk to each other again commenced.

But what good is a conductor without a working hand to conduct? Patrick was determined – several long operations later and endless hours of painful rehab exercises daily saw him back conducting! Even though his hand may never be quite the same again, he can already use each finger, grip paper, and turn his pages on the music score. And, as a virtual post-script, Patrick has just had another operation to right the remaining fingers. Things are looking good. But what got him there? What kept him going? Where did he get the grit to keep at it? I thought I'd put this to Patrick, and here's a potted version of his story.

I recall looking out the window in the hospital after the operation and thinking to myself, what is my future? Will my hand have to be amputated? Will I get an infection in the wound? Will I say I have to get through this? Do I have to succeed? I can't imagine a life deprived of my music, and I recall a rush of unwavering desire to overcome the odds, whatever I had to face — with patience, determination, diligence and passion.

Musicians are trained to overcome challenges with practice and diligence. I had the best medical team imaginable. They had belief in their operation and belief in me, so I knew I would be able to overcome whatever obstacles I faced. If they set me a goal, I was determined to go one better.

Every person and family grapple with a myriad of issues daily, weekly, and monthly, and my mantra has always been that there is a way to solve every problem. Maybe you have to change tack or change your thought processes. You might have to think sideways and learn to adapt. Animals do. They have injuries and adapt, and we're the same. Whatever happens, I have to succeed, and I will learn to adapt just as animals do.

What I got out of this insight into Patrick's profile were the traits of determination, passion and adaptability. It's common to see obsessive-compulsive passion and determination traits, but that style can't adapt. This capacity to tack, weave, and adjust your thinking looms as a key ingredient in Humble Heroes.

Well done, Patrick. I'm proud to call you my friend.

Editorial comment:
"Recovery, resilience, success, failure — these all may circle around our determination. If you think about it, nothing really comes to be if someone isn't determined to make it happen. Work isn't completed, paintings go unfinished, relationships end, healing doesn't happen, and choices aren't made if we aren't determined."
— Sarah Deats, Hope Inc

Story 76

Tahlia

When kids' bad imagination has them petrified,
logic won't work but powerful good imagination
can often do the trick

*J*ust how much are kids absorbing from all their time on their devices? And what impact is it having on their minds and attitudes? I know this concerns all parents and grandparents as we deal with the all-encompassing power of technology.

This story is probably a lesson in being diligent about what kids watch. Tahlia was one of those adorable, wide-eyed, bright kids with a very fertile imagination. She could play by herself and role-play for hours on end. But that imaginative mind had its downside.

I don't know if you remember the movie "Child's Play". I haven't seen it, but I gather it has some rather horrible Chucky dolls with horrible eyes and devouring personalities. Tahlia's parents were wise enough to know that she should not be exposed to anything scary because she internalised it, elaborated on it and made it a monster of the mind. They didn't let her watch "Child's Play", but they didn't count on other parents who might.

Her friend, Hannah, had seen it and was keen to tell Tahlia this graphic story about this Chucky doll, adopted by an Australian couple, whose nails continued to grow. Then during the night, Chucky scratched dad and mum to pieces, so the little girl fled to her aunty's, and the next night, they found her all scratched to pieces too.

Tahlia's mighty imagination did the rest. She could not only see Chucky; she became possessed by it. She would panic if left alone, wouldn't be in her room by herself, and it got worse every night until she couldn't go to her room. This Chucky doll spooked her, so when I met her, she was shaking with fear, and her little eyes were sunken. Even mentioning Chucky by name made her mouth quiver, and she would start to get short of breath.

Her parents said they had tried reasoning, but panic and obsessions are not responsive to reason, so no bribe, punishment or explanation would work. They tried shooing the doll out the window, but Tahlia could see this Chucky doll, and it just hid and came out when they stopped.

Tahlia and I had to get our counter forces operating. As she was pretty susceptible to a good story, I thought I'd have to trump a bad story with a better one. Too often, adults forget that kids are kids. They don't reason as we do; they imagine like we don't.

I discovered that her favourite fluffy toy was Simba, the lion, so we decided that Simba was the most powerful of all creatures, king of the jungle and a great Chucky chewer. Any time Chucky or his clones appeared, Tahlia would call on Simba to "go chew Chucky", and Simba would pounce on him, gobble him up and grin for more.

Tahlia and I practised combining Simba's presence and power when confronting Chucky. We did this a few times till Simba was deadening Tahlia's pain and good magic had outgunned bad magic.

Then, with Simba clutched in her arms, she went off with a grin, ready to do battle.

The message to be gained from this story is to keep an eye on what the kids see, an ear on what they say, and a lap for what they fear.

I bet Tahlia still has her Simba in her life, ready and waiting to devour nasty thoughts or ideas and protect her at night.

Maybe we all need a safety symbol, something like Simba.

Editorial comment:
No "maybe" about it, Dr John. You are right. We all need those places where we feel safe; the secret places, the important places.

"Child of mine
Come as you grow
In youth you will learn the secret places
The cave behind the waterfall
The arms of the oak that hold you high
The stars so near on a desert ledge
The important places
And as with age you choose your own way among the many faces of a busy world
May you always remember the path that leads you back
Back to the important places."
—"Dad for Forest," 1986

Story 77

Duncan

Duncan's dad was neither humble nor, (in the eyes
of his family) heroic, but the ashes test sorted it
out and peace was restored

Podcast Listener's Humble Hero

ere's a listener's story with a difference. It's Fred's story about his brother-in-law's journey from detesting his dad, Malcolm, while Malcolm was alive, to an enlightened re-assessment, literally over the ashes. I've included it because it carries the message that it's never too late to forgive.

Dr John,

This story is not about a hero, it's about the journey of my brother-in-law, Duncan, from detesting his dad to a belated understanding, and the shift came literally over the spreading of the ashes.

My father-in-law Malcolm had chosen the spot where he wanted his and Rose's ashes spread. Rose's wishes were that her ashes be scattered elsewhere. The funeral parlour had retained her ashes. Now it was time to dispose of the mixed remains as per the instructions left behind.

Three of us were overseeing this operation – Duncan, the son, Susan, the daughter and me, Susan's husband. The atmosphere was not cordial when we arrived at Malcolm's preferred spot. Duncan was agitated and just wanted it "done and dusted". I had not seen this side of him at all. He moved towards a clump of bushes. "Let's spread the ashes and go to the pub. We can talk there."

However, when we got to the pub, Duncan's mood changed. I bought a round of drinks and proposed a toast to Malcolm and Rose. As Duncan put his glass down, he said he missed mum but not dad. "Dad always bossed her around. He always bossed everyone around. But I've had the last laugh. I kept some of the ashes. As per mum's wishes, we could bury them properly at the cemetery where we grew up."

Susan and Duncan began reminiscing about their parents. Rose had met Malcolm in the early 'fifties, and his story fascinated her. He had lost a leg in the beach landings on Borneo in 1945. Maybe in hindsight, he had suffered from war-based PTSD.

Malcolm sent the children to boarding school in Sydney when they were old enough: Duncan to a school that would make a man of him and Susan to a place that would turn her into a young lady. The local school wouldn't be able to do either of those things. All the children knew was that Malcolm had always been the boss.

"I hated that bloody school." Duncan almost spat the words out. "I wanted to stay in town, help Pop on the farm, and be with my friends. I hated that school."

Duncan stared into his glass, and the others said nothing. "I loved mum, but there were times I hated dad. He sent us away and made our mum's life miserable. He was always telling me what to do. He was always telling her what to do. He controlled everything. Bastard."

Susan put her arm around her brother's shoulders and reminded him that dad was only 18 when he went into action, and the Japanese soldier who shot him would have killed him if it hadn't been for his best mate, Duncan, who saved him and took a fatal bullet in the process.

They agreed that this experience probably soured dad and may have been why he had become so bossy and challenging.

Duncan mulled over what his sister had said. "Well, I tell you one thing, I've never been afraid to tell my boys I love them. I've let them make their own decisions about what they want to do with their lives. Maybe dad did mean well, and now I have to unlearn what he taught me and do it my way – the softer, more loving way. Anyone for another?"

Rising from the ashes, Duncan had found a new peace and understanding. His mum was undoubtedly still Duncan's hero, but his dad was no longer his enemy. It was a moving moment that I'll never forget.

Editorial comment:
Charles Dickens' childhood was marked by abuse and neglect when his parents sent him, at age 12, to work in a factory. Dickens included an account of this in "David Copperfield", and writing the novel might have helped him forgive his parents. Who knows?

"If you can't forgive and forget, pick one."
– Robert Brault

Story 78

Timmy

Our Timmy's life may have been short but his
legacy lives on in our family

What do you have around the house that your kids, parents, or special friend made or bought for you? Regarding kids' relics, I'm a bit of a sentimental hoarder. I have virtually every Father's Day card any of the girls ever gave me, and in the kitchen cupboard, we have every melamine plate with the kids' (and even a few grandkids') drawings on them, dating back to their preschool days. And we have all their growing-up photos too.

Some photos are sad, especially the one of Timmy, our eldest son, who died as a baby. Timmy had Down's Syndrome and a severe heart problem. He was never able to suckle, and we had to wake him and whirl him around to get him to take even the odd suck or two from the bottle. At that time, Jean worked as a teacher/matron in a school for disabled children, many of whom had Down's syndrome. We had seen the toll significantly delayed children had had on their parents' well-being, so we knew what was in store.

Friends would call in with their young kids to see how we were, and then I would see them heading back up the driveway, hugging their children, as if to say "Thank God, it's not us." Those friends will never know how much that hurt us – sort of using our crisis as a relief that it wasn't their problem.

Then, amid our crisis, I went downtown to get petrol and the guy at the service station, whose wife was in the labour ward with Jean, asked how the baby was. In sombre tones, I told him of the circumstances and health concerns – he just shook his head at me and said, "Hang on mate, you've got a kid, haven't ya? That's all that matters", and maybe that's all that should have, but not to me. I could see my family unit struggling with little hope for any quick solutions, and there was no NDIS then. We were all alone.

So when I saw Jean's feeding difficulties and plummeting self-confidence, I became fearful and resentful. Then because Timmy wasn't putting on any weight, the doctor ordered him back to the hospital so he could be intravenously fed and monitored. We would go in to see him each day, sit by the bed, and just look at each other. Jean looked at me to say she was sorry, she had failed me, and I would look to her with no capacity to comfort and reassure. On our last visit before Timmy died, his sunken eyes seemed to bore through me as if he knew what was in my heart. I can still see that image. I cannot erase it.

So this wasn't a good chapter in our lives, but that experience and the loneliness I felt at that time convinced me to specialise in child development. But even more importantly for my career, it made me committed to supporting every parent who came through my clinic door. Whether the problem was child behaviour or development or parental feelings of inadequacy, I swore none would leave my rooms feeling unsupported, unheard or judged. I hope I did that!

If it hadn't been for Timmy, I would never have been able to help as many as people tell me I did. Good things rose from those ashes just as they do for each of us when we don't know where to turn. Just grab the good things when they do come along and ride out those times when they don't.

Sorry son. I wish I had that time over again – but maybe the lesson for all of us is to make love and forgiveness fundamental cornerstones in our daily lives.

Editorial comment:
That was a harrowing story to read, yet Dr John leaves his sad story on a positive note and references the cornerstones in our daily existence. The cornerstones. The first stones to be laid in a new building. The foundations on which we build.
This brings to mind the cornerstones of faith, hope and love on which people of most religions build their lives.

Love in Hinduism is sacrament. It preaches that one gives up selfishness in love, not expecting anything in return. It also believes "God is love."
"Oh, holy Great flame, Grant me with love."
– Hindu sacred text, Kanda Guru Kavasa.

Author Vs Editor

A light-hearted lesson for the editor that good
outcomes often take devious routes

Behind every book lies the tension between the author and editor. Richard and I have shared great times before and over this book. However, the retired Headmaster seems to be always heading for the moral high ground and sometimes admonishes me for being too flippant or too pragmatic. I'm not starchy enough. Mind you – we're good mates. You may remember this "clash" in an earlier story, "Phillip's Christmas story". If you remember that story, you will have noted that my editor took me to task for my careless attitude to "truth" in his morally superior comment. I sympathised with Phillip, who had to tell his son a white lie to avoid a Christmas disaster. I pointed out that sometimes half-truths and white lies may be forgiven in the pragmatic world of loss and gain to achieve your outcome. I quote my morally superior editor:

> I'm not sure I totally agree with Dr John's summary of this story. I've seen too many examples of where telling a white lie to save the day has led to misery down the track.

Then again, our esteemed Editor took me to task over the mess I got in when caught in a web of half-truths in the story about my secretary Brenda. I quote:

> Walter Scott refers to the memory-shrivelling effects of lying and how one lie leads to others. As the lies multiply, we become trapped in the sticky web of deceit.

And what about Barbara's creative way of solving her granddaughter's hair-pulling problem? In "Barbara shows her ingenuity," Grandma talked her four-year-old granddaughter, Olivia, into wearing her knotted bonnet with a red pom-pom on top to prevent the night-time habit of hair-pulling. Barbara had Olivia convinced that Rudolph and the other reindeer wouldn't stop to deliver Christmas presents if they couldn't see her wearing her bonnet. Despite the lack of research-based evidence, it worked.

Often doctors will use whatever creative or imaginative method comes to mind when dealing with mind-over-matter issues. Here's another story I just read that used shock therapy of a different kind to achieve an effective cure. Please remove your morally superior hat and don your laughter hat before you read on.

> An elderly lady went to the doctor's office, where a very experienced GP saw

her in his white coat. After about four minutes in the examination room, she burst out of the room, tears pouring down her face as she ran down the hall. A female colleague in the practice, noticing her distress, rushed over, put her arm around the patient's shoulders, and asked what the problem was and how she could help. The upset patient told her the story. After listening, the doctor had her sit and relax in another room.

This lady doctor then marched down the hallway back to where her colleague wrote his notes and said, "What the hell is the matter with you? Mrs Terry is 73 years old, has four grown children and seven grandchildren, and you told her she was pregnant?" The examining doctor continued writing and, without looking up, said, "Well, it cured her hiccups."

Richard, as I've said throughout the book, laughter is often the best medicine. So now is your final chance to admonish me and regain the moral high ground. Thanks for sharing.

It has been great fun, and in a world of anger and media-promoted fear, it's good to have a laugh and recharge our soul batteries. But the stories are more than that. As in the John Paul Young song, they are reminders that love is in the air everywhere we look around – we just have to tune in to it every day.

Editorial comment:
What can I say, other than to quote the Bard?
"If we shadows have offended,
Think but this, and all is mended,
That you have but slumbered here
While these visions did appear.
And this weak and idle theme,
No more yielding but a dream,
Gentles, do not reprehend:
If you pardon, we will mend:
And, as I am an honest Puck,
If we have unearned luck
Now to 'scape the serpent's tongue,
We will make amends ere long;
Else the Puck a liar call;
So, good night unto you all.
Give me your hands, if we be friends,
And Robin shall restore amends."
– William Shakespeare, "A Midsummer Night's Dream"

Story 80

Judy

Assistant editor Judy writes an inspirational piece
about her father that shifts the author's attitude
to his own dad

*T*hroughout the podcasts of my Humble Heroes, my grandson, Jensen, and I called for listeners' stories of their heroes. As a proud Scottish descendant, this story had me in tears. It's so beautifully written.

> *Dear Dr John,*
>
> *My Humble Hero was my dad. He loved all things Scottish. He enthusiastically embraced progress but had an abiding love of tradition. And despite being a true-blue Aussie, his Scottish roots stayed with him to his dying day. I wrote this piece at a writing course but resurrected it here after dad died recently and in memory of a much-loved and humble hero.*
>
> *I had read about the clearances back in Scotland in the 1800s. Maybe that's why our Alexander McAlpine of Ayrshire and our Thomas Graham of Fifeshire embarked on a three-masted ship bound for the colony of Victoria, far, far away at the bottom of the world.*
>
> *Maybe that's why dad always played "Jimmy Shand and his Band" on his reel-to-reel tape recorder on a Saturday night as we reeled and locked arms, swirling around the Epping CWA Community Hall. Or why Saturday mornings saw little six-year-old Judy in the Eastwood Masonic Hall, dressed in her Royal Stewart tartan kilt and black lace-up pumps, tentatively negotiating the steps of the Highland Fling. Then, the Sword Dance, leaping into the air and being ever so careful to avoid touching those lengths of silver-painted timber (hardly swords, but hey, it didn't matter).*
>
> *Even today, I can feel my heart pumping and tears welling up as I watch those splendid pipe bands march along George St on Anzac Day. Black Watch tartan kilts swaying, sporrans bobbing up and down, ruddy cheeks swelling, their black ostrich feather hats flickering while "Colonel Bogey" fills my ears and nourishes my heart.*
>
> *And why I also swirl and march around our living room with the grandchildren keeping in step behind me, banging their drums and loudly tooting their little horns and tin whistles in time to "The Scottish Pipes and Drums" pumping out "The Road to the Isles."*
>
> *And so, when the time comes, we will commission a lone Scottish piper to stand at the Church's exit as dad's coffin is carried out by the Jonathan McAlpines and the James Thomases in our family. The piper*

will play "Amazing Grace" and, despite the sadness and the grief, how sweet will be the sound.

As it happened, dad died peacefully, aged 98, while we were in lockdown. So there was no final visit. As my sister held a phone to his ear, I told him how grateful I was for his love and wished him a speedy journey to those hallowed halls.

Dad's ashes came to our farm, and a lovely 75-year-old man from Wingham, in his tartan kilt and regalia, played all the Scottish tunes on his bagpipes as dad's children, grandchildren, and great-grandchildren climbed the hill overlooking the Gloucester valley. And at the end of the Service, as we scattered those ashes, "Amazing Grace" rang out and how sweet was the sound.

Judy, I am proud to include your dad as a Humble Hero. Thank you.

Editorial comment:
There's a Brigadoon-like quality to this lovely, evocative story of Judy's dad. That image of the lone piper playing as the family climbed the hill will stay with me, and I'm sure many readers will feel the same.

"Amazing grace how sweet the sound
That saved a wretch like me
I once was lost, but now I'm found
Was blind but now I see."
– John Newton

Epilogue

These stories of mine are no more special than the humble heroes in your life. If these stories inspire you to acknowledge, embrace and encourage your Humble Heroes, then our little contribution has set us all on a better path for good.

I can't end without a few words that capture the essence of my perspective on life, written by one of my favourite authors, Robert Fulgham, taken from "All I Really Know I Learned in Kindergarten", Grafton Press, 1986.

> *I believe that imagination is stronger than knowledge.*
>
> *That myth is more potent than history.*
>
> *That dreams are more powerful than facts.*
>
> *That hope always triumphs over experience.*
>
> *That laughter is the only cure for grief.*
>
> *And I believe that love is stronger than death.*

May we all die young, as late as possible! Thank you for sharing some of my journey. I hope it has helped you on yours.

About the Author & Editor

Dr John Irvine PhD, MACE, MAPS, has been one of Australia's most heard, seen and read Paediatric Psychologists. He had his one-teacher school at 18, then taught in NSW for many years before becoming a Paediatric Psychologist. Dr John, as he is affectionately known to thousands of families, has worked with children and their parents for 60 years.

He was awarded the Shell Prize for Arts and the University Medal during his honours-level studies at the University of New England. Armidale Teachers' College then appointed Dr John as a Child Development and Behaviour Management Lecturer. Following this, Dr John accepted an appointment to set up Early Childhood Education Studies in Toowoomba at what is now the University of Southern Queensland.

Dr John initiated preschool training in Toowoomba, where he also set up the state's first and most comprehensive family daycare and family support scheme. At this time, he undertook a doctorate in children's play. Upon completing his PhD, Dr John accepted an appointment as Principal Lecturer in the School of Early Childhood in Sydney, thus enabling the family (wife Jean and daughters Jenny, Heather and Rosie) to be closer to their extended family. He had a community house dedicated to his name for services rendered to families in the region. During his time as an academic in Sydney, Dr John commenced his writing career, publishing "Coping with Kids", "Coping with School" and "Coping with the Family". His expertise and communication style attracted the media's attention, and he began his "Coping with Kids" radio series on 67 stations across Australia. Dr John then became a regular writer for a popular family magazine and then a regular on Australian television, including appearances on the Today show, Sunrise and other daytime programs.

After leaving his academic role, Dr John focussed on building the READ Clinic with his brother Warwick. The brothers designed the Clinic to become a one-stop shop for psychological services on the NSW Central Coast. During those years, Dr John updated his previous publications, writing "Who'd Be A Parent: The Manual That Should Have Come With The Kids" and "The Handbook for Happy Families". Material from the latter publication became the content for his four DVDs of "Happy Families". While acting as a consultant on children's play, Dr John discovered Andi Green's WorryWoos. He has dedicated much of his retirement years to promoting their worth in developing children's Emotional Intelligence. Dr John has written two booklets for parents about the WorryWoos: "Helping Children Beat The Worry Bug" and "Helping Young Children Manage Frustration And Anger". He has also written the Australian guidelines for using the WorryWoos in schools and early childhood centres.

The stories are a tribute to all the inspiring people Dr John has encountered in his professional career. He first produced the stories as a series of podcasts but has now put them into print. The stories are mostly about ordinary people, but the occasional celebrity pops up now and again. All the stories are based on real life and are inspirational - each with its unique life lesson. Dr John hopes they will prove as moving and uplifting to the reader as they have been to him.

Richard Lornie OAM, FACE, MA has worked for over 50 years as a teacher, university lecturer, headmaster and consultant – in various settings and three nations: the UK, Papua New Guinea and Australia. For 21 years, Richard was the Headmaster of Central Coast Grammar School (CCGS), and it was there that he first became acquainted with Dr John. Dr John was the visiting education psychologist at CCGS, and he and Richard worked closely together, becoming friends and colleagues. Richard and his wife Lindy live on the NSW Central Coast.